THE RED ROAN RIDER

When an appeal for help arrives at the Bar
10 Ranch, Gene Adams and his two pals
Johnny P .ma and Tomahawk saddle up and
ride. Wh : seems a straightforward case of a
ruthless ancher using his wealth and power
to destro an entire community soon turns
sour, ar 1 the three find they are in a
situatio more dangerous than they could
ever ha e imagined. All seems lost for the
Bar 10 nen. Lost, that is, until a mysterious
hooded horseman rides to the rescue. This
man, rave, daring and incomparable in
streng h, became known as the Red Roan
Rider.

THE RED ROAN RIDER

THE RED ROAN RIDER

by

Michael D. George

Dales Large Print Books
Long Preston, North Yorkshire,
BD23 4ND, England.

British Library Cataloguing in Publication Data.

George, Michael D.
    The Red Roan Rider.

    A catalogue record of this book is
    available from the British Library

    ISBN   1-84262-125-4 pbk

First published in Great Britain 2000 by Robert Hale Limited

Copyright © Michael D. George 2000

Cover illustration © Ben Warner by arrangement with
P.W.A. International Ltd.

The right of Michael D. George to be identified as the author of
this work has been asserted by him in accordance with the
Copyright, Designs and Patents Act, 1988

Published in Large Print 2001 by arrangement with
Robert Hale Limited

Dales Large Print is an imprint of Library Magna Books Ltd.

Printed and bound in Great Britain by
T.J. (International) Ltd., Cornwall, PL28 8RW

Dedicated to
Alex Gordon

ONE

Gene Lon Adams pulled the brim of his black ten gallon Stetson down to shield his eyes from the blinding Texas sun as it hung low against the sugar-loaf mountain range before them. For a moment he just stared out at the merciless panorama as he toyed with his skin-tight black leather gloves. Gene Adams ruled his own domain called simply the Bar 10 ranch like the living legend he was. Yet this was not the Bar 10. This was a place far to the south of his ranch and he was here with only his two most trusted men for company.

To his right stood the cantankerous Tomahawk, whilst on his left, the youthful figure of Johnny Puma. The only two human beings whom Gene Adams totally trusted. They were a long way from the safety of the Bar 10 ranch which was reputed to be the largest spread in all of the Lone Star State. They were not here to sightsee, but on an errand of mercy.

Neither of the three riders had ever ventured this far south of their ranch before, but when Adams had received the letter from his old friend Brook Ward, from a small town called Sanora, thirty miles north of Corpus Christi, he did not hesitate in saddling up and riding. Tomahawk and Johnny had tagged along as they always did, knowing they would eventually be informed what was up.

Gene Adams was a man of indefinable years. His white hair seemed to defy the youthful looks of a face which sported black eyebrows set amid a rich golden tanned skin. To all who knew him he had always appeared the same. Neither young nor old. Sitting atop his magnificent chestnut mare he was obviously the leader of this trio of men. Adams rode as he lived, solidly, wearing his famed pair of golden guns in their hand tooled holsters.

Tomahawk was a very different kettle of fish. Sitting on his black quarter horse he appeared to be well past his prime yet had enough sparkle in his eyes to denote a character who still had some tar left in his brush. Bearded and sparse of teeth, he seemed to have been around forever. Still capable of getting himself into scrapes like the rascal he was, Tomahawk wore a gun which he seldom used yet was never without his trusty Indian hatchet – a weapon he handled expertly.

Riding his sleek pinto pony, Johnny Puma followed wherever Adams led, like a dutiful son. For over six years the young man had lived and worked on the Bar 10. He was now a skilled rancher but it had not always been so. Once there had been another life now far behind him. A life which relied upon his skill with his Colt Peacemakers. A life which might have ended long ago had it not been for Gene Adams. Adams had given him a new life and a new name and Johnny

Puma had never forgotten his debt. A debt he had repaid a hundred-fold over the years but which he still felt obliged to honour.

Brook Ward was a man to whom Adams owed many a favour over the years. A true friend who had risked his own skin on Adams's behalf more than once. Adams always repaid his debts whatever the cost. Apart from Johnny and Tomahawk, Brook Ward was the only other man ever to get close to the rancher.

The three riders were heading south because of Brook Ward's letter. Tomahawk and Johnny still did not know the contents of the note that had spurred Adams into action so swiftly. Where he led, they followed. When Gene Adams rode, they rode too. When he deemed it time to explain, they would listen.

Reining up, Adams sat tall in his Texan saddle as the dust swept past them out across the barren landscape towards the setting sun.

'We oughta make camp, boys,' Adams suggested.

Tomahawk looked around them at the arid land they had found themselves in.

'You sure, Gene?'

'You ain't gonna start belly aching again, are you?' Adams dismounted and stared at the bright red sky ahead of them as the sun began to dip below the distant sugar-loaf shaped mountains.

Tomahawk hoisted his right leg over his horse's neck before sliding from his mount. Mumbling as he removed his bed-roll from behind his saddle cantle Tomahawk began to make camp as instructed. This was a place where scorpions raced across the ground and the old timer knew it. Bedding down here was like taking a bath with a sack full of diamond-back rattlers in your lap.

'You ever been to this Sanora before, Gene?' Johnny asked as he eased himself off his saddle.

'Nope,' Adams replied as he watched his men starting to make camp. 'But I've heard tell of the place.'

'How come you are so fired up by old

Brook's letter?' the sultry face of Tomahawk questioned.

Gene Adams gazed at the sand and its deadly creatures. He untied his bed-roll and tossed it to the old man.

'When a friend is in trouble, you gotta help. Right?'

'Reckon so,' Tomahawk nodded.

'Get a fire going before it gets dark, boys,' Adams said.

'Ain't gonna be too hard getting a fire going around here, Gene,' Johnny remarked as he pulled a lifeless handful of dead grass from the ground. 'I reckon everything around here is dead and tinder dry.'

'Expecting the scorpions,' Adams pointed as one of the deadly creatures scurried past them.

Tomahawk removed all three of their saddle ropes and began muttering to himself as his friends looked on.

'What are you doing, Tomahawk?' Adams finally had to ask.

'These lariats are made of horse hair,'

Tomahawk replied.

'They are?' Johnny shrugged.

'Yep. They are.' Tomahawk began carefully laying the lariats on the ground around each of their bed-rolls.

'So?' Adams stood resting his gloved hands on the grips of his golden guns.

'It just so happens that *vaqueros* down south of the border reckon scorpions don't like horse hair and won't cross over a lariat laid around a bed-roll.' Tomahawk nodded knowingly.

Gene Adams looked at Johnny and winked.

'I heard tell up in Montana, pixies ride on the backs of butterflies, Johnny.'

'Well ain't that darn interesting, Gene?' Johnny Puma leaned over the old man.

'You boys figure on gathering up some kindling so we can gets some vittles into our bellies or are ya just gonna keep giving me lip?' Tomahawk stomped his foot angrily on the dry ground.

TWO

The night had been even colder than Adams had predicted as every ounce of heat evaporated from the ground around them. Their mounts had been tied firmly by their reins to each of the men's saddlehorns beneath their heads. Even so, the horses had been troubled like their masters by this place. A place of death.

Daybreak saw the three Bar 10 riders heading still further south into a land alien to them as its satanic heat began to rise with every passing hoof beat. Here even the scorpions appeared to hide from nature's fury. Deeper and deeper into the cruel landscape the trio rode.

This was no place for people. Devoid of anything remotely fashioned by the hand of civilization their journey had begun to take on sinister proportions. The vastness of the Bar 10 seemed to employ all of nature's strange quirks but nothing like this place. They were heading further and further into a region which no sober human should ever investigate but Adams continued leading them on.

It was roughly noon by the tortuous sun which seemed directly above their heads when Adams reined in and stopped his mare. All three men dismounted and watered their horses using their Stetsons as makeshift buckets.

'You've been awful quiet, Gene,' Tomahawk remarked.

'Yep,' Adams agreed placing his wet hat back onto his head.

Tomahawk knew the look in Gene Adams' face. He had seen it many times over all the years they had been together.

'When are ya gonna tell us what's in that darn letter?' The old timer rubbed his chin as if attempting to flatten down his wild whiskers.

Adams stared thoughtfully at his empty canteen before screwing on its stopper and returning it to the saddlehorn.

'We ride another two miles toward that mesa and there's a spring according to old Brook.'

'Ain't a saloon anywhere around here is there?' Tomahawk grinned.

'Only a spring full of crystal clear water,' Adams grinned back.

Johnny Puma and Tomahawk looked at one another before nodding in unison. It sounded fine.

'Brook's letter must be mighty important to get you so all fired up, Gene.' Johnny Puma rubbed his brow with his shirt sleeve.

All three men mounted once more and headed in the direction of the distant mesa. It was as if their three mounts could smell the water as they thundered across the steadily rising ground.

The spring of water was exactly as described in the letter from Brook Ward, which Gene Adams finally pulled from his coat pocket and began to read to his two friends.

August 15th. Sanora.

Dear Gene,
It troubles me to have to write to you, old friend. Yet I see no way out of the pickle I've found myself in. If it were only me in a jam, I'd try and muddle through but there's my wife Bessie and Anita, my daughter, to consider. It's hard to know where to begin but I guess the trouble started brewing about a year back after the spring round up. As you know I have been building up my herd of cattle since buying my own small ranch. Everything was going fine until a man named Rufas Johnson moved into the south Texas plains with a bunch of roughnecks. He secured a large chunk of the best grazing land for himself which spanned the Nueces River. Soon there was not enough water flowing through the plains and our stock began to die of thirst.

We found out Johnson had dammed the river. We have tried to meet with Johnson to no avail. Then Indians began raiding our ranches killing stock and anyone who got in the way. Gene, I need help. We all need help.

Your friend,

Brook Ward.

'When a varmint starts to hog water from his neighbours, it's tantamount to murder, Gene,' Tomahawk mumbled over his beard.

'No wonder you dropped everything to help,' Johnny said as he handed the letter back to Adams.

'This Rufas Johnson character sounds a calculating hombre.' Adams folded the paper before returning it to his coat pocket along with the map.

'Is it legal?' Tomahawk began filling the spare canteens from the spring.

'Reckon so,' Adams' eyes narrowed. 'Legal but not what I call exactly moral.'

'I don't get it.' The old timer scratched his whiskers.

'Get what?'

'The part about the Indian attacks.'

Gene Adams nodded in agreement. 'That's the one thing which has been gnawing away at my craw too, Tomahawk.'

'What kinda Indians are down there, Gene?'

'The last I heard there wasn't any Indians down there.' Adams raised a black eyebrow as he stared at the bubbling water which kept on coming from out of the ground. 'I heard they all headed west to richer pickings a long while back.'

'What can we do?' Johnny moved closer to the older men.

'Johnson might be skimming the edge of the law by his actions and so will we.' Adams pulled the tight leather of his left glove as he flexed his fingers. 'I've been around a long time and there ain't many rules I can't figure on bending when I've a mind to; and I've a mind, right now.'

'Why would anyone do such a thing, Gene?' Johnny asked as he watched the thoughtful features of the man who had become like a father to him.

'In these parts, water is more valuable than gold, Johnny.'

Tomahawk nodded in agreement.

'Water is power and if you've got all the water...'

'Exactly. You have all the power.' Adams rubbed his chin.

Gene Adams stood and beat the dust off his pants with his Stetson before placing the black hat back onto his head. 'I wonder if it's a coincidence that suddenly Indians show up and start killing just when this Johnson character has been causing havoc.'

'It don't figure, Gene.' Tomahawk replaced the stoppers on all their canteens and rose to his feet beside the sturdy rancher.

Gene Adams placed a hand upon the older man's shoulder.

'You're dead right, old timer. It don't figure at all.'

The three men from the Bar 10 had ridden for another ten or more miles when they pulled their mounts up at the sight which loomed ahead of them. Dust was rising into the still blue sky along the flat top of a mesa.

'You see what I see, boys?' Adams said holding his reins to his chest as he stared hard at the sight.

'Riders,' Tomahawk nodded.

'A lot of riders by the amount of dust being kicked up.' Johnny Puma swallowed deeply.

Tomahawk turned and looked at Adams. 'Reckon it could be them Indians Brook wrote you about?'

'Maybe.' Adams wrestled with his nervous chestnut as he studied the lay of the land ahead of them.

'What we gonna do?' Johnny asked.

'We ride wide.' Adams pointed to their left.

'That looks like mighty tough terrain,

Gene.' Tomahawk wiped his face on his sleeve.

'We've ridden through tougher.' Adams pulled his reins and spurred his mount into action.

The three men rode hard across the dry baked ground trying to give the imposing mesa a wide berth. Heading their mounts into the very heart of the ferocious landscape Adams led his two men cautiously. What at first had seemed a good plan, now began to unravel like the fibres of a spent lariat. Soon they found themselves amid a forest of high cacti and cruel bushes covered in razor sharp thorns which tore at their clothing. After only a few minutes, Adams pulled his horse to a stop with his two companions following suit only yards behind him.

Adams was not a man who admitted defeat easily but staring around the scene the Bar 10 rancher finally turned his chestnut mare full circle to face his men.

'There's no way through this!' he exclaimed. 'Even a rattler would have trouble getting through here.'

'That means we have to ride over that dang mesa,' Tomahawk gulped.

'I don't like it.' Johnny shook his head trying to think of an alternative plan.

'I ain't exactly bursting with relish at the idea myself, Johnny. But it's the only way.' Adams rode between the two men slowly checking himself for wounds as he headed out onto the scorched ground once more. Reining up as his friends drew level he watched as the swirling dust whipped up into the cloudless sky seemed to be getting closer.

Adams stood in his stirrups. 'They've spotted us, boys. Head for cover.'

The ground around their mounts suddenly came to life as the noise of the rifle fire filled their ears. Adams spurred hard and began to race across the foot of the mesa firing with one of his gold-plated Colts as he held his reins loose allowing the mare to find its own speed with his free hand.

Tomahawk's quarter horse burst into action beneath his ragged britches and soon outpaced the large chestnut as he too fired with his free hand up at the mysterious horsemen atop the high ground.

Only Johnny Puma seemed either unable or unwilling to risk his hide by riding across the open sun-baked ground for the distant cover where his two companions were heading. Dismounting, he slid his Winchester from its long holster and cranked its mechanism faster than he had ever done previously. Firing up at the dust where his keen eyes could see the bright flashes of carbine discharges, he knew he had the better of their attackers. Before he had let his final shot go from his trusty long rifle, he could tell these were not men who liked being pinned down by an expert with a gun such as himself. For a moment he paused, wondering whether to reload his weapon, then he slid the rifle back into its sheath before swinging up onto his saddle. Kicking the pinto pony hard, he raced across the dry ground towards his now motionless part-ners. Hauling the pony to a halt he raised a hand to his eyes and stared up at the high dust.

'It looks as if the dust is thinning,' Tomahawk said as he screwed up his old eyes trying to see as they stared out in the direction of the sun.

Adams agreed, holstering his gun. 'They are definitely heading away all right, old timer. That was fine shooting, Johnny.'

'Thank you kindly, Gene. Reckon it's safe for us to carry on?' the youngest of the trio asked.

'Safer than trying to ride through that thorn forest.' Adams rubbed the neck of his horse before looking at his men in turn.

'We oughta take it a mite slower than normal, Gene,' the old rascal advised. 'I'd hate for us to catch up with them critters.'

'I agree, Tomahawk,' Adams smiled wryly. 'Johnny sure gave them call to be a tad angry with us.'

'How come they wouldn't open up on us?'

'I guess it's just another mystery, Tomahawk,' Adams replied.

Tomahawk spat at the ground. 'I don't cotton to the taste.'

'Me neither, old timer. Me neither,' Adams drawled.

Once again the three riders of the Bar 10 began to approach the mesa. This time they were holding their reins in check so their horses did not reach its summit too quickly. They wanted to allow the other riders plenty of time to be gone. As they rode, Gene Adams checked his gold-plated pistols and indicated to his two friends to follow suit. Whatever lay ahead upon the rocky plateau gave him good cause for concern. They were now in another man's domain and Adams knew it. This was no place to get caught out in the open. Death lurked here.

It had been a steady slow ride which none of the three had any stomach for. Fools might rush in where angels feared to tread but these men were neither. Only the words in Brook Ward's letter kept them heading forward. Words which none of them could either forget or ignore. Men such as Ward did not ask for help easily. It was not their way. To ask for assistance was tantamount to admitting a flaw in one's manhood. When such a plea was given, men of the same grit like Gene Adams and his companions, could never refuse to help. However much their own deep-rooted fears ate at their innards they kept on riding towards the danger because there was no other way.

Men faced their fears head on. Only cowards were deaf to another man's problems.

THREE

When their horses had scrambled onto the top of the flat mesa all three riders stopped and dismounted. The horses were given rest and water as the riders moved around studying the scene. Only Tomahawk had any true knowledge of tracking and was quick to work his way around. Even now, forty years past his prime, there was nobody to match his skill at finding tracks where none seemed visible.

'It weren't Indians, Gene,' Tomahawk said firmly.

Adams stood watching the experienced old timer as he knelt and stared at the ground. Tomahawk's eyes were fixed on the hard rocky surface beneath his fingers.

'Not Indians?' Gene Adams leaned over and looked at the ground which seemed too rough to give up clues to any untrained eye.

'These horses were shod.' Tomahawk looked back at Adams and pointed at something only he could see and interpret.

'I see nothing, old timer,' Adams admitted as he strained his vision attempting to locate the signs his friend had found.

'I do.' Tomahawk stood and gazed off to the west where the riders had headed.

'How many? How many riders do you reckon were here?' Adams asked.

'Ten or more riders,' Tomahawk replied.

'Riding shod horses?'

'Yep.'

'You certain about that?'

'Yep. I might not know much but I know what I know.' The old man pulled out his trusty tomahawk and ran a thumbnail along its honed deadly edge. 'I can be certain it weren't Indians because they were riding shod horses.'

Gene Adams patted his friend's back.

'You ain't never made a false call in all the years I've known you, Tomahawk.'

31

Adams and Tomahawk turned and faced Johnny who stood beside their horses that were drinking from out of their upturned hats.

'Young Johnny is scared, Gene,' Tomahawk noted as he slid the hatchet back into his belt. 'I reckon this ain't the sort of job a cowboy like him is used to.'

'Guess that only proves how smart he is, Tomahawk.' Adams rubbed his chin as they slowly walked back towards the horses and their friend.

'How come?'

'It takes brains to be scared.'

'I'm scared too, Gene. Does that make me smart?' Tomahawk gave a huge sigh as he felt a wave of doubt over their mission overwhelming him.

Adams laughed out loud.

'You're the smartest old scallywag on the Bar 10, Tomahawk.'

The town of Sanora lay roughly two hundred miles north-east of Laredo on the banks of the Nueces River. A small town made up of white-washed adobes for the most part with only a thin scattering of more recognizable Texan style structures. Lying on the banks of the once full waterway, surrounded by farms and ranches, Sanora was now vulnerable. Once pirates had sailed their four-masters up past Corpus Christi and used the natural inlet to rest from their pursuers and divide their plunder. Later on refugees from Mexico had found Sanora a virtual paradise from the horrors of a continually warring land south of the Rio Grande. Then came the Texans and for several decades the town served its people well. Just a simple ordinary Texan cattle town.

Until the fateful day when the river began to dry up and die. That was the day Sanora also began to die. Slowly at first, then each day saw the water levels dropping faster and faster until the once wide lush life-giving river had become a mere dried up bed of cracking mud.

It was the surrounding cattle ranchers who first noticed the precious liquid diminishing until their herds began to die of thirst. It happened quickly. Very quickly.

Soon fresh water could be obtained only from the wells in town and on the various ranches. Most thought nature was inflicting its wrath and for some reason the south Texas plains had been struck by a drought but soon it became obvious that this was no cruel act of nature. This was the act of one man. For whatever reason, Rufas Johnson was behind their plight and the sudden appearance of a strange band of marauding Indians who were torching the tinder dry farms only added to the local people's anxiety.

As the three riders from the Bar 10 entered the town of Sanora they could not believe their eyes. It was clear this had once been a town worthy of distinction but now it was visibly dying: not just its buildings, but its people.

FOUR

Tiberius Fox was a man who seemed to look exactly like his odd name implied. A strange mass of red hair with white flecks edging his sideburns certainly gave the old sheriff the look of a sly woodland creature. His was an unobstructed view out of the open office doorway down the long dusty street at the three approaching riders. As the three riders from the Bar 10 drew their mounts up outside his office and dismounted, Fox stood and walked out of the open doorway onto the creaking boardwalk to greet them. His was not the usual appearance ever to greet Gene Adams from behind a star. Dressed more like a riverboat gambler than a peace officer, the slender-framed sheriff studied the trio intently. The rancher paused before handing his reins to

Johnny Puma as he stepped up onto the porch before removing his hat.

'Sheriff,' Adams said trying not to stare at this most unusual of human beings before him.

'Name's Fox. Tiberius Fox. Who might you be?'

Adams ran a hand over his mouth as the name found its mark.

'They call me Adams. Gene Adams. These are two of my most trusted men. Tomahawk and Johnny Puma.'

'Adams of the Bar 10?' Fox asked as he studied the men in turn.

'You've heard of the Bar 10 in these parts?' Adams beat the trail dust from his chaps with his ten gallon hat.

'Big ranch. Too big for its reputation to be diluted by distance.' Fox moved to the edge of the porch and leaned against the wooden upright. 'You boys are a heck of a long ways from home. How come?'

Adams's two friends moved to either side of him as he watched the sheriff staring out at the sun baked town.

'I heard tell you've got trouble in these parts.' Adams stepped closer to the thin man.

Fox turned his head and looked at the square-jawed features of Adams who was replacing his hat over the snow white hair.

'How would knowledge of our troubles reach the Bar 10, Adams?'

Adams rested his gloved thumbs in his belt. 'Brook Ward wrote me.'

Fox's expression suddenly altered as the name penetrated his mind.

'Brook Ward?'

'What is it?' Adams stepped closer. 'When a tanned man's face suddenly goes white, it ain't a healthy sign.'

'You're as smart as they say you are, Adams,' Tiberius Fox shook his head.

'I'm waiting for answers, Fox,' Adams said in a hushed expectant tone. 'I'd be obliged if you would…'

'Brook is dead,' Fox said through gritted teeth.

For a moment Gene Adams felt as if he had been kicked in his stomach. He moved around the man with red hair silently before gazing up into his two friends' faces.

'Brook is dead?' Adams repeated the sheriff's words in disbelief.

'We're too late!' Johnny snarled angrily at the brilliantly bright sky.

'How did old Brook die, sheriff?' Tomahawk asked.

Fox looked up at the three men.

'Killed by Indians. Last night on his way into town.'

'Indians?' Adams rested a gloved hand upon the sod wall of the sheriff's office and frowned.

'Why?' Johnny Puma questioned the lawman.

'A lot of folks have been killed by Indians around here lately. Who knows why.' Fox walked sorrowfully into his office with the three men close behind him.

Adams watched as Fox seated himself. 'How do you know it was Indians?'

Fox opened the top drawer of his desk and pulled out a long arrow, its tip covered in dried blood.

'I don't know much about Indians but this is an Indian arrow, ain't it?'

Tomahawk accepted the arrow and moved to the doorway before studying it carefully.

'Apache?' Adams asked the older man.

'Nope. It ain't Apache.' Tomahawk looked up at the other men inside the office.

'Then who?'

'I ain't ever seen no feather flights like these before, boys.' Tomahawk tossed the arrow back to the seated sheriff who caught it expertly.

'Not Apache,' Adams mumbled to himself.

'I thought I knew the way every darn tribe made an arrow but that one is a mystery to me, Gene.' Tomahawk brooded. 'I can't figure it out.'

Gene Adams leaned over the desk and looked down into the face of the sheriff who seemed as puzzled as they all were.

'Would you take us to where our friend died, Fox?'

Tiberius Fox stood and moved to the crude hat rail where his Stetson hung. Plucking it from the rail he placed it upon his head before strapping on his simple gunbelt. As he buckled it and leaned down to tie the leather lace around his left thigh his expression changed.

'Follow me,' he said stepping out into the sunlight.

FIVE

The ride from Sanora had taken the four men due east. It was a trail littered with the rotting carcasses of literally dozens of steers. Not a welcome sight to cattlemen, however hardened they were. This had once been prime grassland and still echoed its recent history in the few shaded places beneath trees. Now the grass had become brown and scorched as the ground water evaporated through its cracked surface, no longer fed by the great river.

Adams had been silent since leaving the town and steering his chestnut close behind the sheriff, Tiberius Fox. Adams simply could not imagine why anyone would have killed his lifelong friend, Brook Ward. Some men challenge fate by their selfish manner but not Brook. He had been

41

one of life's gentlemen.

Now as they were nearing the spot where the murderous act had occurred Gene Lon Adams felt sick to the pit of his empty stomach. Tomahawk had drifted at the rear of the four riders clutching his hatchet in one hand as he steered his black mount with the other. He had watched each and every possible hiding place with a keenness of eye many younger souls would have envied. He knew an ambush was a possibility and was ready to warn his younger companions at the first sign of danger.

Johnny simply rode as young men always do when troubled by news their minds found hard to comprehend. His was the innocence of youth. Death was never a welcome visitor and having struck Brook Ward down, it had come too close.

Fox led the group with an almost military precision. Never pausing his horse's pace one iota. Never looking to either side of the long dry trail. Always staring straight ahead as if transfixed by their destination at all costs.

The three Bar 10 men reined in when the sheriff raised his arm and slowed his horse to a standstill. Drawing level with the law officer they encircled the spot he was pointing down at.

It was an ordinary-looking piece of dried up sod but the blood which had baked into it chilled each and every one of the riders as they gazed at it.

Gene Adams was first to dismount from his chestnut mare and walked around the fatal spot thoughtfully. Nobody knew the memories which drifted into his mind as he recalled his old friend whose blood was now part of the ground before his boots.

'Tomahawk?' Adams said forcefully.

The old man slid from his saddle and edged towards the tall rancher rubbing his beard sadly, as he took great care not to step onto the stained ground.

'What you thinking, Gene?'

Adams waved his arm around at the parched terrain which surrounded them.

'Look for tracks around here, old timer.'

'If there are any here, Gene. I'll find them,' Tomahawk began to scan the surrounding area like a hound seeking out the scent of a racoon.

'What's wrong, Adams?' Fox asked as he took a swallow from his canteen.

'This Indian thing don't sit well on my craw, Fox,' Adams replied as he paced along the trail and stared out into the distance.

Fox jabbed his spurs into his horse's body and moved the animal closer to the Bar 10 rancher.

'You seem a mite suspicious.'

'I am,' Adams agreed glancing up briefly before returning his attention to the skilful Tomahawk.

'How come?' the sheriff asked, screwing the stopper back onto his canteen.

'Indians coming back to a place they quit years ago?' Adams raised an eyebrow. 'Then they decide to start killing. Why? What would they hope to gain?'

'Maybe they've been paid,' Fox surmised.

'Paid to kill,' Adams nodded at the idea.

'Who do you reckon would pay a bunch of Indians to do his killing for him, sheriff?'

Fox sat still in his saddle as if either unwilling or unable to offer an answer to the astute question Adams had posed.

'How far off is the spread belonging to Rufas Johnson?' the Bar 10 rancher continued.

'Thirty miles due north,' Fox pointed. 'I hope you ain't thinking that Johnson is behind this, Adams?'

'I ain't thinking nothing, Fox. I'm just weighing this damn mess up trying to make some sense out of it.' Adams spat on the ground.

'Johnson ain't been linked to any of the incidents which have struck our community,' the nervous sheriff added.

'Not yet,' Adams glared.

'I hope you ain't considering taking the law into your own hands, Adams?' Tiberius Fox rubbed his eyes with his long coloured bandanna as he spoke.

Gene Adams gave a knowing look up at

the lawman.

'Where's Brook's place?'

'A few miles up this trail,' replied the lawman, aiming a finger in the general direction.

'This sure ain't a good place to die,' Johnny muttered from atop his pinto pony.

'There ain't no good places to die, Johnny,' Adams noted aloud. 'Only sad ones.'

The young man nodded in agreement as he moved anxiously in his saddle, carefully looking out for any hazards which might be lurking there amid the dead grass.

Gene Adams watched as Tomahawk carefully moved back towards them, still staring at the ground.

'Find anything, old timer?'

'Hard to say, Gene.' Tomahawk removed his hat and rubbed a hand over his head.

'Any useful tracks?'

'Plenty of tracks – but whether they have anything to do with the killing is hard to figure.' Tomahawk grabbed at his reins and stepped into his stirrup before mounting the placid animal.

'Any unshod tracks?' Adams asked when he walked back to his waiting mare.

'Not a single one.'

Adams paused as he heard the statement. He looked up at Tomahawk before turning to the quiet sheriff.

'Not even one?'

Tomahawk shook his head.

Mounting his chestnut, Adams turned his mount to face Tiberius Fox squarely.

'Don't you find that a tad curious, sheriff?'

'The ground about here ain't the best to find tracks in at the best of times, Adams,' Fox shrugged.

'True. But if Tomahawk can't find something he's looking for, it ain't there.' Gene Adams moved his mount beside his two men and bowed to the lawman.

'I'm heading back to Sanora,' Fox stated. 'You boys heading back now?'

Gene Adams stood in his stirrups and stared up the trail for a moment before narrowing his eyes.

'Not for a while, sheriff. We've gotta pay

our respects to Brook's widow and daughter first.'

'Suit yourselves. But be careful when you decide to head back because this land is crawling with vermin.' The red-haired sheriff turned his horse and spurred the animal into a gallop back to town. The afternoon sun was heading on down towards the horizon once more. Fox was wise enough to know this was no place to be after dark.

'And the vermin ain't necessarily got red skins.' Adams tipped his hat at the departing sheriff who was still riding straight and true like a military cadet on parade.

'You trust that hombre, Gene?' Tomahawk asked.

'Hard to say, old timer,' Adams shrugged. 'I think he's a man who never thought evil would raise its head in his backyard.'

The three riders from the Bar 10 headed along the trail. The same trail which their friend had taken the previous day on his last fateful journey.

The home of Brook Ward and his small family was modest by Texan standards but perfectly suited the man himself – solid and well-designed with no frills.

The glowing sun had now blanketed the sky crimson as it began to set. The three riders carefully entered the small fenced yard before pausing their lathered up mounts beneath the hand-painted sign which declared this was the 'WARD RANCH'.

'Bessie? Bessie Ward, this is Gene Adams come a-calling!' Adams yelled out at the house.

They watched as the door was carefully opened and a cautious female stepped out holding a carbine across her bosom.

'Is that really you, Gene?' Bessie Ward shouted back holding the palm of her hand up against the sun's dying rays.

'It is, darling.' Adams stood in his stirrups and removed his black hat to reveal his hair.

'It is you, Gene.' She shouted. 'I'd recog-nize that snowy white hair anywhere. Come on up to the house. I won't shoot you.'

Adams gave his men a quick glance before urging his chestnut mare forward up to the house.

'Was she serious about shooting, Gene?' Johnny asked as he steered his pinto alongside the mare.

'Yep. That's one lady who can shoot a carbine better than most men,' Adams replied as they reached the hitching rail and trough outside the doorway where the short rotund female waited.

As Adams stepped down from his mount she rushed into his arms and began sobbing. He said nothing as he tried to comfort her grieving with his gentle hands around her back. Then all three men's attention was drawn to the open doorway once more as an incredibly beautiful female stepped out into the sun's crimson farewell and approached them silently.

Gene Adams looked over Bessie's head at the young woman who seemed to be in her late teens.

'You don't recognize me, Uncle Gene?' Her voice was as soft as her skin.

'Anita?' Adams queried. 'Is this little Anita, Bessie?'

The sobbing woman stepped away from the tall rancher and dabbed her eyes with the edge of her long apron as she nodded.

'My little Anita ain't so little any more.'

Gene touched her face with his gloved hand.

'You got your mother's looks, Anita.'

'Thank you for coming, Gene,' Bessie said leading the men into her home.

'Sorry we arrived too late to help Brook, Bessie,' Gene sighed regretfully. 'We tried our best to get here as fast as our horses could bring us.'

'You came and that's what matters.' The voice of Bessie Ward was beginning to regain its composure.

Gene Adams turned to Johnny and Tomahawk.

'These are my two best hands, Bessie. Tomahawk and Johnny Puma.'

Bessie grabbed Tomahawk's whiskers gently. 'I remember Tomahawk, Gene. He hasn't changed a bit in all these years. Still as handsome as ever.'

The old man suddenly went coy.

'Can we stay here tonight, Bessie?' Adams asked the small round woman. 'I reckon it's safer for all of us if we do.'

'Certainly, Gene,' Bessie Ward agreed turning to her daughter. 'Anita, show the boys where they can put their horses.'

Johnny moved eagerly forward smiling.

'I'll tend to horses if Miss Anita shows me where the barn is, Gene. You and Tomahawk can rest up.'

Gene raised an eyebrow.

'Why that's darn decent of you, Johnny.'

Bessie watched as her daughter led the still smiling young cowboy out into the court-yard before turning to look at her old friends with a knowing expression upon her face.

'He seems a nice lad.'

Tomahawk began to chuckle.

'Wish I had half his vinegar, Bessie.'

'Reckon he's just fallen in love again, Bessie,' Adams laughed. 'Remember how easily it was to fall in love when we were that age?'

She nodded.

'I remember, Gene.'

Tomahawk sat down at a table and started unbuckling his dusty chaps. 'I recall falling in love when I was young, Bessie.'

'Was she as beautiful as my Anita, Tomahawk?'

'She weren't a female person, Bessie. She was a golden palomino mare. Sixteen hands high if she was an inch. I loved that horse.'

Gene Adams removed his black Stetson and hit the old man across the back of his head.

'Sometimes I worry about you, partner.'

SIX

It had been a good, if simple, meal which Bessie Ward had served her guests. After eating on the trail since leaving the Bar 10 the three visitors began to feel their humanity returning once more. Leaving her mother inside to recall happier times with her friends, Anita had slipped out onto the porch to sit beneath the canopy of stars. Silence had been her only companion since learning of her father's death. A silence which came from within her heaving breasts and beat to the pounding of her broken heart. The stars which twinkled brightly against the backdrop of a jet-black sky somehow soothed the young female's mind. A mind still incapable of coping with the reality of her loss. She had not shed a single tear since hearing of her father's brutal killing and knew it was not natural. Yet her eyes remained dry like their land.

'May I join you, Miss Anita?' came the question from Johnny Puma's nervous lips.

Slowly Anita turned and looked up at the tall handsome cowboy as he hovered in the doorway anxiously.

'If you like, Johnny,' she heard herself saying.

He did not require a second invitation and closed the door before moving beside the chair where she rested. It was dark out on the porch. It was impossible for either to see one another clearly and yet they sensed each other's presence as if it were a bright midday bathed in sunshine.

'This is a nice spread,' Johnny said softly.

'It was a nice spread once. Not any more, now it's dead like most of our prized stock.' There seemed to be an emptiness in her words.

Johnny edged his way around the lovely Anita inhaling her natural perfume deeply into his soul.

'Gene will fix things, ma'am,' he told her as he sat on the edge of the porch beside her small naked feet.

'It won't bring my pa back, Johnny,' Anita sighed.

Johnny knew she was correct but felt he and his friends could make things better than they now were.

'You had any trouble here on the ranch?'

'What sort of trouble, Johnny?' Her voice was like melted butter as it swept over the cowboy.

'Anyone try to give old Brook a hard time?'

'Nope!' she blurted out trying to find the place within her which was still capable of feeling emotion. 'Until last evening everything was OK. Our stock had been dying through thirst and lack of grass to fill their swollen bellies but the Indians had not attacked us. Not until last night.'

'Even then they chose to bushwhack your pa down on the trail rather than striking here on the ranch itself, Miss Anita.' His words had somehow managed to hit the nail on its head.

'Come to think about it, I've never heard of Indians who bushwhacked folks.' Anita leaned forward in her chair.

'It don't make no sense.' Johnny shook his head as if he ought to be able to find answers for this tortured soul. Answers which were beyond his understanding. 'Robbers bushwhack folks to steal their money and suchlike. Not Indians.'

'Pa wasn't robbed, Johnny,' Anita added thoughtfully.

'Indians attacking a single rider after sundown just don't seem right.' Johnny could now see her teeth and eyes sparkling in the light of a hundred thousand stars.

Then they heard a noise out in the blackness beyond the courtyard fencing. Suddenly both the youngsters felt an unease filling their spines with ice.

'What is it, Johnny?' Anita's voice was trembling.

Johnny rose to his feet and thumbed his gun hammers as he squinted out into the darkness.

'You hear that, Anita?' He whispered as she rose beside him.

'I heard something, Johnny.' Her voice was pitched as quietly as his own. 'I'm kinda scared.'

Johnny Puma knew the darkness prevented him from seeing his prey clearly but it also gave Anita and himself equal protective cover.

Then they heard it again. A rustling sound which seemed to travel from one corner of black horizon to the next beyond the fencing. Standing in the shadows Johnny Puma drew both his Colts and cocked their hammers in readiness. Then he felt her firm body pressing into his back and her breath against his neck.

'What is it?' she asked softly into his ear.

'Could be them Indians,' Johnny replied, as sweat trickled down his face. 'Maybe they reckon it's time to finish the job they 'started last night.'

'Look!' Anita exclaimed as they both saw two figures racing past the barn.

'I can't get a bead on any of the varmints!' Johnny drawled angrily under his breath.

Trying to concentrate Johnny stepped down from the raised porch and moved closer to the side-panelled wall. With each step he felt Anita's body pressing into his back. She seemed glued to him and totally unaware of the effect it had on the trail weary cowboy starved of female company.

Then Johnny's keen vision saw movement to his right as someone ran towards the corral and the solid barn.

'Was that a critter or a man?' she asked.

Aiming high, Johnny squeezed the trigger on his right hand Colt and watched as the man-made lightning tore across the yard and soared over its target, violently taking the tip off a fence pole, sending a million burning splinters into the air.

Anita tugged at his shirt causing the cowboy to look at the house as Bessie, Gene and Tomahawk extinguished the oil lamps hurriedly.

Then Johnny heard a noise which chilled him to the marrow: the sound of an arrow hurtling through the night air as it sped in their direction. Dragging Anita down onto her knees they made it just in time as the arrow drove into the side walling of the house and the young man fired again.

Rushing out into the darkness, Gene Adams raised both his golden guns. Before his eyes had time to adapt to the darkness, the rancher felt the heat of an arrow passing too close for comfort. Falling onto one knee he screwed up his eyes until he could see a target and let go with two shots from his left pistol.

'Stay inside, Tomahawk!' Adams yelled at the house.

'Must be them Indians, Gene!' Johnny shouted as he shielded Anita with his own body.

Firing again at the fencing, Adams knew they had no targets and only guesswork to guide their bullets.

'Can you get Anita indoors, Johnny?'

'I'm kinda pinned down, Gene,' Johnny said as he angrily fired four more shots out at their invisible enemy.

Finally Gene Adam's vision began to adjust to the dark chilling courtyard. He could see movement racing across beyond the fence poles and fired once more. This time he heard a shriek as one of his bullets found its target.

'You got one of them critters,' Johnny said as he began to edge Anita back toward the doorway. Then they heard Bessie's voice echoing.

'Keep your heads down 'cos I'm letting rip!' she bellowed.

The feisty female stood in the door jar and began cranking the mechanism of her trusty Winchester and firing. The sheer speed of her skilful handling of the carbine amazed all three men as she peppered the outlying fence poles with bullets.

Anita sat on the ground with her fingers in

her ears as the lead from her mother's rifle lit up the darkness. Its lethal cartridges tore through the cold air above their heads in well-grouped volleys. There were few women who could handle a Winchester as capably as Bessie Ward. She had learned her skills whilst still a young child on a wagon train travelling west with her folks. By the time they had reached the Texas Pine Woods her family had been reduced from nine to a mere three, but the skill remained.

Johnny tried to see what was going on as suddenly a wave of arrows flew across the open ground and filled the wall above their heads.

'How many are there, Gene?' Tomahawk called from a window to the rancher.

'Too many, old timer,' Adams yelled back. 'Stay with Bessie and load her carbine.'

'What about me using one of our rifles, Gene?' the old man called out.

'She's a better shot than you, Tomahawk.' Adams crawled towards the two pinned down youngsters.

'I don't like it, Gene!' Johnny said before firing wildly out at the darkness again. 'They got us nailed for sure if we can't break out from here.'

'We stay here, Johnny,' Gene ordered. 'It would be suicidal for any of us to move out there.'

'But…'

'They've got us cornered, boy.' Gene helped move the young girl back towards the house as Bessie gave them cover with another volley of lead over their heads. There was another scream as one more bullet appeared to find its target.

Scrambling on all-fours, the trio managed to crawl back into the relative safety of the house past Bessie's broad legs.

Gene Adams got to his feet before moving beside Bessie Ward and staring out over her shoulder.

'Good shooting.' He patted her back fondly as she lowered her weapon and moved back into the house.

'They got us well and truly pinned down,

Gene,' she sighed.

Adams moved closer to the doorway and gazed out.

'We got at least two of them.'

'How many does that leave?' Tomahawk quizzed.

Adams shrugged. 'Too many, Tomahawk.'

'I never known Indians to attack at night like this before,' the old tracker said in disbelief. 'Can't be Apache. Not even old Cochise would be willing to upset his tribe's Gods like this.'

'Whoever it is got us trapped, old timer,' Gene Adams said as he emptied the spent cartridges from his pistols onto the floor.

'Is there a back way out of here, Bessie?' Johnny asked as he held onto Anita's arm.

'I'm afraid not, Johnny,' the woman answered. 'Brook never saw the need for one.'

'In normal circumstances there wouldn't be call for one, Bessie,' Gene comforted.

'Trouble is, these ain't exactly normal circumstances, Gene.'

'What do they want?' Anita said loudly.

'I reckon they want us dead,' Bessie replied.

'But why, ma?'

Bessie Ward shook her head unable to think of an answer to her daughter's question. Maybe there wasn't an answer which made any sense to the five trapped people within the farmhouse but out there in the darkness, someone knew why. Someone had all the answers.

Then the Bar 10 rancher's eyes widened as he saw something which chilled his blood.

'What's wrong, Gene?' Bessie Ward asked as she noticed the expression alter on her friend's handsome face.

Adams pointed. 'Look.'

They all did as he instructed and looked out into the yard where a fire was being lit amid the dry brush.

'Now we can pick them off easier,' Johnny smiled as he moved to a window and pulled open its solid wooden shutter.

'Wrong, boy,' Tomahawk corrected.

'What do you mean, old-timer?' Johnny could not understand the concern amongst his friends.

'Fire arrows, Johnny,' Adams swallowed deeply as the words left his dry lips. 'They are gonna start using fire arrows to burn us out.'

SEVEN

Gene Adams and his companions stood watching helplessly as the fire grew in intensity, sending rolling flames up into the cold night sky. The images of figures were fleeting as they moved around beyond the boundary poles of the courtyard, like phantoms tossing tinder-dry brush onto the flames to feed its fury. Never quite in one place long enough for any of the trapped quintet to take aim at; never remaining stationary for more than a few fleeting seconds, taunting the ensnared onlookers into wasting their precious ammunition.

It was as if Adams and his friends were watching something from another time as the flames spat out in all directions like a mustang when first shown a wrangler's rope. This was no normal fire built to keep people warm. This was a fire created to kill.

'What's taking them so long, Gene?' Tomahawk mumbled through his beard as he stood beside the tall Bar 10 rancher. 'They could have started to shoot their fire arrows at us by now. They are playing with us.'

'Ain't like an Indian to taunt his victims,' Gene Adams said as he held onto his gold-plated pistols firmly staring out at the troubling vista.

'Why don't they stay in one place long enough for me to take aim?' Johnny snarled as he rested his Colts on the open window sill. 'I still reckon I ought to try to make a move on them with my guns, Gene.'

'Easy, Johnny,' Gene nodded as the fire's ferocity began to illuminate the interior of the farmhouse. 'Stay calm and stay alert.'

'What we gonna do, Gene?' Johnny's voice begged for the mature advice he knew only Adams could muster. 'I could get close enough to kill at least a few of them before they got me.'

'Reckon you're still a crackshot, Johnny boy?' Adams stared out at their enemy as he spoke.

'I reckon so. Why?' The young man's face seemed to suddenly come to life as he began to believe the rancher had thought of a plan which just might save their bacon. Johnny knew if anyone could, it was Gene Lon Adams.

'Figure you could shoot down flaming arrows from the sky?' Adams posed his question calmly and watched as the youthful looks of his young friend turned toward him open mouthed. 'Well? Do you think you are that good a shot?'

'It can't be done, Gene,' Johnny said.

'Maybe it can't but I'm gonna try,' Adams's face was like carved marble as he spoke.

Bessie had just finished loading her Winchester as she sat beside her daughter at the table. 'I figure we might have to try, Johnny.'

The young cowboy looked at the smiling

woman and then at her beautiful daughter.

'It would be one heck of a turkey shoot and no mistake, ma'am.'

'Everybody make sure your weapons are fully charged because we ain't gonna have time for no reloading when it starts,' Gene Adams sighed. 'Tomahawk?'

'Yeah, Gene?' The old man moved even closer to the boss of the Bar 10.

'Your job is to keep them carbines loaded and make sure me and Johnny don't run out of shells.'

The bearded old timer nodded.

'You can rely on me, Gene.'

'I know I can.' Adams gently tugged at the man's whiskers as he rubbed the sweat from his brow with the back of his gloved hand.

EIGHT

Then it started. It was as if the sky was raining with fire. The arrows, having had their lethal tips wrapped in dried grass, were dipped in the flames just long enough to catch alight. Then they were fired high into the air towards the farmhouse. A few at first which Adams and his companions managed to divert with their deadly accurate bullets, building up in volume with every passing second. Each of the fiery missiles were diverted from their chosen target by either Adams, Johnny or Bessie's accuracy.

All three knew that to miss even one of the blazing arrows would result in the dry house being set alight, forcing them out into the courtyard to be slain by their still unseen enemy.

As Adams discharged one pistol he

handed it to Tomahawk who quickly reloaded it, whilst the rancher used his other. Anita sat between Johnny and her mother with a box of rifle cartridges in her lap, loading the rifles Tomahawk had missed during the confusion. The air was thick with choking gunpowder and the acrid smell of sulphur after only a matter of a few deafening minutes. Minutes which seemed to last hours in the pounding hearts of all five trapped souls as they fought for their very lives.

Suddenly, without warning, the onslaught of lighted arrows ceased and gunfire could be heard coming from beyond their line of sight behind the now dying fire. Gunfire not aimed at Adams and his friends, but at their attackers.

Adams screwed his eyes up as he tried to see who or what was firing a weapon out there on the parched plain. For a moment the Bar 10 rancher thought about Tiberius Fox before quickly dismissing the image. Fox had been scared of being out here after dark by his own admission. Yet who else would come to their assistance?

As the big man desperately attempted to make sense of the frantic chaos which now dominated the scene beyond the fence poles, he felt Tomahawk grabbing at his forearm.

'What's going on, Gene?'

'I've no idea, old timer,' Adams admitted as he cast an eye over at the others who were looking equally confused.

Then Adams noticed horses. Many terrified horses being led in and mounted by the Indians. Adams tried to work out from where the gunfire was emanating, but there was too much dust and smoke billowing around the scene to make out anything clearly.

Adams carefully aimed through the flames and saw one of the long haired men falling as his bullet met its target. He felt no satisfaction in his accuracy and lowered his pistol. Bessie moved over to the kneeling Adams and rested a hand upon his shoulder as if she were trying to listen clearly.

'Do you hear that, Gene?' she asked.

Adams turned to the others. 'Everybody hush up for a while.'

Through the thick blanket of smoke which now obscured everything apart from the dying fire, horses could be heard frantically whinnying as more shots rang out in the still night air. Horses which then thundered out into the darkness away from the Ward ranch.

Gene Adams slowly rose to his full height and edged his way out into the yard which was filled with sparks from the bonfire's final moments. With each step, the smoke seemed to become less dense.

As Adams cautiously moved further away from the house with his four friends in close attendance, he felt his heart beginning to steady itself as the sound of horses galloping away rang in his ears. A welcome sound which he had feared he would never hear.

Just as he had slipped his two gold-plated Colts into their fine holsters a startling figure on horseback rode from around the corner of the house and reined to a halt before him.

Adams stood before the magnificent stallion in utter amazement. This was no ordinary rider, the rancher thought.

This was a man unlike any other he or any of his companions had known before.

Gene Adams stared in wonder at the sight which he knew had chased off their attackers.

The fire still had enough spirit left to illuminate the strange rider before them. Dressed all in dark crimson with a mask beneath his Stetson which completely covered his features, the man sat proudly holding the reins of his muscular red roan stallion, looking down at the five people through two neatly cut eye holes. For an instant, Adams had thought the Devil himself had ridden in from the fires of Hell, yet this was no evil spectre before them. This rider had been their saviour for no apparent gain to himself.

'Who are you, stranger?' Adams asked.

The rider did not reply.

Although Adams had never seen one of these rare horses before, he had heard a lot about them. The animal was a mixture of large white markings with patches of equal sized red swirling patterns and a dark red mane and tail. This was a red roan and truly an animal of majestic stature that the mysterious rider sat upon.

Adams studied the man more intently. On his left hip, the rider wore a handsome Colt Peacemaker with a pearl handle grip, whilst on his right he wore a coiled bullwhip suspended from his gunbelt by a silver hook. The black saddle was even grander than Adams's own with its silver diamond decoration and high silver-tipped saddlehorn. Whoever this masked rider was, Adams thought, he was like his stallion: unique.

'I thank you for helping us, stranger,' Adams said.

Once more there was no reply from the masked rider.

Adams raised an arm and stepped between the rider and his companion's weaponry as if to shield him from their bullets. He instinctively knew this rider was on their side. He had already proven that by his valiant actions.

'Nobody fire on this man!' Adams commanded loudly.

The rider touched the brim of his hat as if silently thanking the rancher.

'Who are you, stranger?' Bessie Ward asked.

'Why the mask?' Johnny Puma stepped beside Adams.

'Sometimes folks wear a mask because they have to, Johnny,' Adams said quietly.

'Outlaws wear masks, Gene,' Tomahawk sniffed.

The rider stroked the dark flowing mane of his mount as he sat listening silently. All five could see the eyes of this quiet man through the small mask-holes beneath his Stetson as the dying fire's light traced his profile. They were not the eyes of a cruel killer shielding his identity from the curious, but more the eyes of a person who like themselves had a mission. A mission which forced him to disguise himself.

'This man is no outlaw, old timer,' Adams said confidently as he studied the eyes.

'Then how come he don't speak, Gene?' Anita asked as she fearfully gripped Johnny's arm, unable to take her eyes off the rider. 'I'm scared.'

'Maybe if he spoke we'd recognize his voice and maybe he just don't want anyone to know who he is, Anita.' Adams stared up at the masked man as if he were able to read his intentions through the disguise.

The rider nodded down at the Bar 10 man.

'What sort of horse is that, Gene?' Johnny asked in amazement at the unbelievably unique stallion. 'I ain't ever seen a horse like it.'

'If I ain't mistaken, it's what they call a red roan, Johnny,' Adams replied. 'I heard tell Jesse and Frank James both ride black roans but this is the first red one I've set eyes upon.'

The rider allowed his stallion to rear up proudly onto his back legs and stretch its forelegs out at the fire's final embers before turning the beast around and aiming its spirited head at the gate. Pausing, the rider tipped his hat once more and then galloped away from the scene.

Gene Adams stood watching the rider disappearing into the darkness until only the sound of distant hooves could be heard on the night air. Suddenly he felt as if they had an ally in the rider upon the red roan who, like them, would fight against injustice and assist in their mission to bring the water back to parched lands around Sanora.

'Who was that?' Bessie asked again.

'That was a rider on a red roan, Bessie,' Adams said walking back to the farmhouse. 'I guess you could call him the Red Roan Rider. Whoever he is, he sure scared them Indians off and saved us all from being roasted alive.'

'Red Roan Rider? I'd sure like me a handle like that, Johnny,' Tomahawk told his young pal as they all followed Adams and the others back towards the farmhouse.

'Skinny Old Black Horse Rider?' Johnny laughed as he walked with his arm around Anita.

'Don't sound too good, does it?' Tomahawk shrugged.

'It would suit you though,' Adams said loudly as he too began to chuckle.

It was ten after three in the heart of the night when the remaining riders entered the well-guarded gates leading to Rufas Johnson's ranch. This land was lush and green as it lay above the massive dam which stretched across the wide Nueces River and had swollen into a virtual lake spreading onto Johnson's lower pastures. A dam made up of a thousand felled trees. Each one laid down with only one purpose: to destroy all who lived south of his property. To anyone who did not know Johnson's purpose in doing such a selfish thing, it may have seemed the act of a maniac but he was no madman. Johnson had a reason for everything he did even though he would not willingly share his motives.

The eight be-draggled riders aimed their mounts along the damp trail which wound through the rich pasture land up to the well constructed house. A house built with the blood money from a different place, a different time. Few had ever set eyes upon the man with the imposing name and ruthless scruples. Few but his own army of rannies. Men drawn from darker places who did his bidding with never a second thought as long as the price was right. The price was always right. Johnson had learned one thing early in his life, and that was how to keep your men happy. He paid big money and supplied all the liquor and female company they required. These were men who would go up against Satan himself to please Johnson. Why? Not through any feelings of loyalty, but simply because he paid their price.

Johnson stood beside his top henchman Burl Nunn on his wide whitewashed porch beneath a line of illuminated lanterns, watching the men returning down the torch lined trail.

'Eight,' Johnson said. 'I count only eight riders, Burl.'

'Should be eleven, boss,' Nunn confirmed.

'How come there are only eight coming back, Burl?' Johnson stepped down and moved towards the approaching riders trying to keep his vast midriff within the confines of his silk vest.

'Must have hit trouble,' Nunn mumbled rubbing his unshaven chin.

'What kinda trouble? I sent them to burn out an old woman and her daughter.' Johnson was agitated by the sight of failure and had his eyes fixed upon the eight riders with failure tattooed across their darkened faces.

Burl Nunn strode down after his employer toying with the grip of his Remington.

'Easy, boss. We ain't heard the facts yet.'

Johnson grabbed the bridle of the first horse to him and watched as the rider slid off wounded. A blood-stained shirt-front greeted the heavily lidded man's eyes as he studied his returning army. They had been defeated, yet it seemed beyond the realms of possibility.

'What happened to you, Clancy?' demanded Johnson of the man who had defeat carved in every pore of his darkened skin.

'Them women weren't alone, boss!' the man gasped as the true extent of his wounds became evident and pain rushed through his body.

'Explain,' Johnson demanded as his man slumped onto his knees in agony as blood seeped from his wounds.

'There was a lot of guns there, boss.' Clancy spat a mouthful of blood at the soil beside his knees. 'I thought we were just gonna make a fire and send in a dozen blazing arrows into the house. Leave them to roast in their own gravy, but there were men there who opened up on us.'

The remaining riders drew their mounts up beside the sweating rancher as he loomed over Clancy Easton's crippled frame. Rufas Johnson watched as they all slid off their lathered horses. At least four others were bleeding and unable to do little except fall onto their knees next to Clancy. The men still able to stand were little better as their faces were racked with confusion at their failure to execute Johnson's orders.

'Who were they?' Nunn asked another of the men angrily.

'I don't know. Whoever they were, they were good with their weapons,' the man responded. 'They pinned us down and took out Harper, Cole and Hardy. We got a fire going but they were damn good shots, Burl.'

'But you had them cornered,' Nunn snarled. 'How come they got the better of you all?'

'The masked devil turned up again.' Clancy sighed as he finally succumbed to his wounds and crashed face first into the dirt splattering blood across Johnson's highly polished boots.

'He came in at us from off the prairie. We were caught in the middle,' one of the other wounded men mumbled. 'He looked like the devil as he came at us cracking that bullwhip and firing his gun. It's his lead we are carrying, Burl.'

Nunn closed in on Johnson, his face ashen even in the glowing torchlight about them.

'Him again. The critter on the roan.'

Johnson waved more of his men from their posts around the house to come and assist the wounded as he turned and strode back towards his impressive house. He walked slowly as suited his build but each step was carefully placed as if hammering nails into angry thoughts.

'Who is he? Who in tarnation is he?'

'This makes three times he's turned up to spoil our plans, boss.' Burl Nunn removed his hat and beat it furiously against his long legs. 'We would have finished it by now if not for that pest.'

'I want that masked roan rider found and

killed, Nunn,' Rufas Johnson commanded.

Nunn nodded. 'I'll kill him personally.'

'After I've cut a slice off his hide to hang on my fence posts,' Johnson growled as he ascended the steps back onto his porch. 'I want his skin peeled off his bones and tanned in the sun before you kill him.'

Nunn spat at the ground. He liked the idea.

NINE

Gene Adams had not managed to sleep a wink since the violent encounter. His eyes had remained wide open until daybreak as if waiting for yet another attack. His companions had slept without knowledge of his silent vigilance. Bessie Ward and her daughter Anita shared a room with two loaded Winchester rifles. Johnny Puma had reluctantly taken to his bed-roll before the large open fireplace where blazing logs had warmed his weary body. Even youth could not battle against fatigue.

Old Tomahawk had snored throughout the remaining hours of darkness upon the long soft cushion covering the wooden breakfast bench, blissfully unaware of Adams's unease.

Adams watched as the sun broke across

the small ranch and the sudden warmth hit him full on as he stood up on the porch. He lifted a Colt from his holster with his gloved left hand and began to move out towards the fence poles which had acted as a barrier between their attackers and the sleeping people within the farmhouse behind his broad shoulders. With every step the smell of smoke grew stronger in his nostrils. The fire had died long ago but it still puffed out its smoke defiantly into the new morning sky.

Gene Adams paused as he got to the long line of poles which still bore the marks of battle. It appeared as though every single pole had been torn apart by their bullets during the brief if deadly battle. Pulling back the gun hammer until it locked into place, he studied the scene carefully for clues which had not been obvious during the frantic attack.

Carefully stepping through the poles, Adams gazed across at the body lying where it had fallen behind the ashes. Then he followed the fence towards the two other stricken bodies lying within the corral. Glancing up, he felt a sense of relief all their horses were uninjured within the stable, unlike the two bodies before him.

Leaning upon the top fence pole, the Bar 10 rancher stared down at the dead Indians and shook his head sorrowfully. He had never taken any gratification from killing, however justifiable it seemed at the time.

'You brooding over these dead Indians, Gene?' Tomahawk's voice caught his attention and forced the tall man to peer over his sleeve at the yawning man approaching from the house.

'Nope,' Adams lied. 'I'm just a tad sleepy.'

'I done seen me a heap of redskins in my life but not like these critters.' Tomahawk slipped through the poles and crouched down beside one of the bodies.

'They look like Apache by the clothes.' Adams released the hammer carefully before holstering his gun and stepping toward the old man as he expertly inspected one of the corpses.

Tomahawk turned his head and stared up into Adams's face.

'Wrong, Gene.'

Adams leaned over until their noses almost touched.

'Then what are they?'

Tomahawk pulled the black wig from the head of the body revealing a balding white man.

'Face is covered with a mixture of grease and colour, Gene.'

Adams strode to the other body and grabbed at the black mane which came off as easily as the one in Tomahawk's hand.

'White men?'

'Exactly.' The old man got to his feet and stared across at the confused rancher. 'White men making out they is Indians. I thought that arrow's feathers didn't make sense yesterday.'

'That you did, old timer,' Adams nodded. 'You ain't nearly as dumb as you look.'

Tomahawk briefly smiled before the true

meaning of his friend's words struck him.

'We gonna take these critters into town for that sheriff to look at, Gene?'

'Reckon so.' Adams gave a huge sigh as he saw the three stray mounts grazing nearby. Bareback horses.

The pair marched back to the body lying next to the ashes of the fire and studied the ground carefully.

'Look, Gene.' Tomahawk pointed at the ground which was chewed up. 'Shod horses.'

'These men deliberately used bows and arrows to convince us all they were Indians,' Adams frowned. 'I imagine they could have opened up on us with carbines but that might have given the game away.'

'It don't make any sense, Gene,' Tomahawk shook his head.

'It does if you look at it from a different angle, old timer.'

'What different angle?'

Adams moved close to the bearded man who kept a firm grip on the Indian hatchet tucked in his beaded belt.

'What if you are a rancher who is trying to clear the land of all other ranchers and homesteaders?'

'Like this Rufas Johnson varmint?' Tomahawk waved a hand in the air.

'Yep. Rufas Johnson.' Adams nodded. 'I bet he got mad when his damming of the river didn't force all the settlers to quit and leave. Mad enough to come up with this idea. Sending out men disguised as Indians to tip the scales in his favour.'

'But why, Gene?' Tomahawk shook his head as he tried in vain to imagine the evil brain behind such deeds.

'He might not want the Texas Rangers to pay him a visit for murdering his neighbours, Tomahawk.' Adams gritted his teeth and ran a gloved hand over his face.

'Yeah. Indians on the warpath don't bring the law down on you,' the old man surmised.

'We know the man must be pretty well-heeled to have bought as much land as he did when he arrived in Sanora,' Adams thought aloud. 'Maybe he just wants to own the entire thing. Some men are just damn greedy.'

'Greedy enough to kill?'

Adams raised an eyebrow. 'You're right, Tomahawk. There just has to be something else. Something I ain't figured out yet. Something which is driving Johnson to act the way he is.'

'I could track them horses back to where they came from, Gene.' Tomahawk scratched his beard.

'After we've seen the sheriff, maybe we'll take us a ride.'

'A ride which I bet leads us to Rufas Johnson's spread.'

They looked across at the dry acrid plain which had once been lush green pasture land filled with thriving steers. Both men then thought about the stranger who had frightened their attackers off, a man who had been masked for some reason neither of them had yet to discover.

As a yawning Johnny Puma stepped out

into the daylight he was greeted by two smiling men.

'Hi, boys,' Johnny said placing his hat upon his head to shield his eyes from the bright sunlight.

'Just in time, Johnny,' Adams said as he stepped through the fence poles and began walking towards the youngster with the old man at his side.

'For what, Gene?' Johnny asked innocently.

'There's a few stray horses scattered about which you can round up and put them dead bodies on.' Adams smiled as he passed the young man.

'On my own?' Johnny queried.

'Of course not, Johnny.' Adams smiled over his shoulder as he and Tomahawk headed eagerly for the smell of breakfast cooking inside the farmhouse.

'You gonna help?' Johnny shouted.

'Sure. Me and the old timer will be out presently,' Adams laughed, 'once we've had our breakfast.'

'You can feed our horses too, Johnny!' Tomahawk shouted as he removed his hat.

Johnny stood open mouthed as the two men disappeared into the house before looking over at the bodies that were lying beside their black wigs within the corral.

'You ain't been scalping these bodies, have you?' he heard himself asking as his throat went dry. 'I ought to get up earlier.'

TEN

Sheriff Tiberius Fox stood beside his two youthful deputies, Jim Jones and Dick Smith, watching as the two veteran Bar 10 riders led the trio of horses down the long dust swept main street of Sanora. Fox moved to the edge of the creaking boardwalk and narrowed his eyes as he focused upon the three lifeless bodies hanging limply over the backs of the bareback animals.

'Who in tarnation is that, Tiberius?' Dick Smith asked.

'Bounty hunters?' Jim Jones queried.

'Nope. They ain't bounty hunters.' Fox stepped down onto the street, resting his wrist on his solitary left hand gun grip.

'Then who?' Smith repeated.

'That there is Gene Adams and his buddy

Tomahawk,' the sheriff informed the younger men.

'Adams from the Bar 10?' Jones suddenly became interested and followed Smith down to Fox's side.

'The very same.' Fox struck a match and put the flame to a long twisted cigar and inhaled the smoke slowly.

'What they doing in Sanora?' Smith could not take his eyes off the pair of riders who were steering their horses directly towards them.

'They come to help Brook Ward,' Fox replied as the smoke filtered through his teeth.

'But old Brook is dead.'

Tiberius Fox nodded. 'Adams ain't gonna let a little thing like death prevent him from keeping a promise.'

Gene Adams pulled his reins up to his chin and stopped his chestnut mare from advancing. He sat waiting for the black quarter horse to draw level with him before dismounting and walking up to the three law officers.

'Where's your young pal Johnny Puma, Adams?' Fox asked the tall mature rancher.

'He's guarding the Ward woman, Fox.' Adams took in a deep breath. 'Folks around these parts seem to require a tad more protection than you're able to provide.'

'My resources are stretched to breaking point, Adams.' Fox blew smoke out at the ground which seemed to preoccupy his attention. 'I do my best with what I've got and I ain't got an awful lot these days.'

Removing his black ten gallon hat to beat the dust off against his chaps Gene Adams stared at Fox until the man looked up.

'These vermin attacked the Ward ranch last night, Fox. They tried to burn the place to the ground.'

Fox and his two men moved towards the three horses carrying their lifeless cargo and checked each of the heads in turn. The sheriff shook his head as he failed to recognize any of the three.

'Why the faces covered in colour and grease, Adams?'

Adams pulled out the three black wigs and tossed them into the sheriff's hands.

'Seems like they were trying to make it look like an Indian attack but they didn't reckon on me and my boys being there to help Bessie and the girl. Not that old Bessie needs much help when it comes to using a Winchester.'

'Whoever these bastards are, only the Lord would know,' Fox said in a frustrated tone.

'The Lord and whoever was paying their wages,' Adams added.

Fox stared at his two deputies and introduced them to the white-haired rancher as he thought long and hard about the troubling situation.

'Dick and Jim here have only just gotten back to Sanora. I sent them to check out the district to see if any other farms and ranches have been attacked,' Fox informed the Bar 10 men.

'Have there been any other attacks, Fox?' Adams's voice was aimed straight at the lawman.

'A few,' Fox admitted.

'All south of the dam on Rufas Johnson's ranch?'

'Yep. All south of the dam, Adams.' The sheriff knew what the rancher was getting at and felt as if salt were being rubbed into an open wound.

Adams sat down on the porch and watched as Tomahawk watered their mounts at the trough whilst the two young deputies led the three bareback horses down toward the undertaker's office. Fox walked up to the seated Adams and looked down at him grimly.

'So this whole Indian thing has been a fake?'

Adams shrugged. 'Yep. The whole thing has been staged to divert attention from something bigger.'

'Staged? By who?' Fox held his cigar staring at the smoke as it drifted into the hot air.

'That's what me and old Tomahawk intend finding out.'

Fox watched as the restless rancher stood once more and placed his hat upon his head before moving to his drinking mare and gathering up his loose reins.

'You still harping on about Rufas Johnson, Adams?' Fox remonstrated. 'I could go making accusations just like you but the trouble is I'm bound by the law. You gotta have proof when you wear a star.'

Adams placed his left foot into his stirrup and pulled himself up into his saddle.

'I can't prove nothing but if it's him behind the murder of my friend Brook Ward, I intend to seek justice.'

'You better not take the law into your own hands, Adams,' Fox warned the rancher as he watched Tomahawk climbing into his saddle beside his friend. 'I know you are a big man up on the Bar 10 but that don't cut no ice around these parts.'

'Understood, Fox.' Adams turned his horse away from the trough and sat staring at the funeral parlour where the two deputies were carrying the bodies. 'I figure

Brook's funeral will take place soon. When exactly?'

'Ten in the morning, Adams,' Tiberius Fox responded sorrowfully. 'I was gonna ride out and tell Bessie and Anita later...'

'I'll inform them.' Adams pulled the leather of his gloves tight over his hands as he toyed with his reins. 'I'll also pay for the entire funeral.'

Fox sucked in his cigar smoke and watched as the rancher's gloved hand withdrew a gold coin from his jacket pocket and handed it down. Fox accepted the coin and placed it into his vest pocket silently.

'Those boys of yours, Fox. Did they travel together?' Adams asked thoughtfully as he remembered the image of the stranger who had come to their assistance during the attack at the Ward ranch.

'Nope. Dick went east and Jim went south.'

'Either of them boys ride a red roan?' Gene Adams raised his eyebrows as he asked the question.

Fox looked up at Adams. 'A what?'

Adams looked directly at the red-haired man. 'A red roan. Does either of your deputies ride a red roan?'

Fox shook his head.

'Dick has a sorrel and Jim uses one of my horses. A grey mare.'

Gene Adams cast a look at his old friend and indicated they ride. Turning their mounts around to face the dusty trail which had brought them here, they spurred. Riding slowly down the long street past the funeral parlour and out over the raised river embankment the two men found themselves in the deep rut which once flowed with the river's precious fluid. Now only a meaningless trickle ebbing through its middle, it was cracked and dangerous. The two men reined in and stared up the almost dry riverbed for a few moments before mutually deciding to continue. Their destination seemed inevitable as if decreed by an unheard voice. Gene Adams and Tomahawk steered their horses upstream to the place they knew would lead to the tracks of the fleeing riders who had vainly tried to burn down the Ward ranch. From there, they were certain, it was merely a matter of time before they would be led to the Johnson spread and its dam. Neither rider spoke as they cautiously rode along the dead river-bed.

ELEVEN

Johnny Puma stared thoughtfully out at the land beyond the fence poles and the shimmering heat haze which obscured his vision. Out there only a handful of steers remained where once an entire herd had roamed with the Ward brand on their hides. Johnny could feel the noonday sun on the crown of his Stetson and the sweat running down his spine beneath his dusty shirt. This place was dying before his very eyes. Only the buzzards, which circled above fallen steers, had any reason to be thankful. Without water to irrigate the soil and feed the roots of the thin Texas grass, it seemed only a matter of time before everyone's bones would be picked clean and bleached white. Death was lurking just beyond the Joshua trees and Johnny could smell its evil hanging on the still dry air.

The deep well barely coped with filling the trough beside the stable and he was thirsty. Yet he rationed his thirst knowing each mouthful which passed over his lips deprived the women and the stock. He rubbed his sore eyes with his shirt sleeve trying to make sense of the baked scenery before him. Why would anyone knowingly destroy this or any other place? he pondered. Texas was as big as anywhere he had ever been and surely big enough for all who settled in its vast land. Greed was doing this and it had to be stopped somehow. Johnny knew, if something could be done, Gene Adams would do it.

Leaning upon the splintered fence poles, Johnny felt a helplessness overwhelming him. He was fast with his Colts and yet knew bullets could not cure this devastation. Only water and plenty of it would restore nature's delicate balance to these lands. Then he heard something. Behind him, came the rustle of Anita's long cotton skirt as she walked bare footed towards him. Johnny turned. Staring from beneath the wide brim of his hat at the vision moving towards him, he found himself smiling.

'What's wrong, Johnny?' Her voice sounded soft as it left her beautiful lips.

'I'm worried,' he admitted freely.

She moved to within an inch of him and looked up into his face and returned his smile.

'You are a pretty good-looking critter, Johnny. For a cowboy, that is.'

'It must be the heat,' he said trying to control his feelings as he soaked up her perfume. 'You ought to wear a hat in this heat, Anita. A gal can go loco if she gets too much sun, y'know.'

She stepped closer. Now her body rested against his and she liked the feeling.

'You gotta girl back on the Bar 10, Johnny?'

Johnny tried to back away but found the fence poles against his spine and her warm body pressing against his front.

'Ain't many girls back home. Not pretty ones anyway.'

'Am I pretty, Johnny Puma?' Her lashes were dark and beat like the wings of a delicate butterfly.

'Oh you're darn pretty.' He felt her body pressing through his shirt and jeans and it felt fine. Mighty fine.

'So you're single?'

Her faultless grin disarmed him.

'I … I … I am kinda unattached, I guess,' he gulped.

'What's wrong, Johnny?' She was now teasing her prey with every gift at her disposal, and she had a lot of gifts.

'Nothing's wrong,' Johnny said clearing his throat. 'I figure you are just kinda lonely stuck out here in the middle of nowhere and me being a man and you being in a state after last night and all…'

She had him. Before he could continue his feeble attempt at being noble, she had him. First her arms had his shoulders. Then her fingers had his face and finally her lips had his lips. He tried for almost two seconds to fight her off but it was a vain and useless attempt. She had wanted to kiss him and he found she tasted even better than she looked. And she looked fine.

When she released him, Johnny seemed to sag as if drained of all air for a moment. He had never been overcome by a female like this before and was dazed and more than a little flattered.

'You taste nice, Johnny Puma!' she exclaimed as she pulled herself off him and walked back towards the house. 'Better if you shaved though.'

Johnny could still feel the impression of her firm breasts against his tingling flesh beneath his shirt front as he watched her disappearing back into the building. He had kissed a lot of girls over the years and never found himself unable to speak afterwards, until now. Now he just found himself slumped against the poles of the corral with his mouth open. Whatever had been troubling him before she kissed him was now a distant memory. All he could think about was Anita Ward. Her body and her face and her taste. She was apple pie on legs, he thought. Apple pie with cinnamon and sugar on top.

It was an imposing structure by any standards. Imposing but vulnerable. Gene Adams and his faithful sidekick Tomahawk had spotted the wooden dam from five miles away. They had also seen the sunlight bouncing off the long rifles of the men perched along both sides of the river's dry embankments. Men paid to do little else but kill anyone or anything venturing too close to the man-made structure. Knowing they themselves had not been observed, the two Bar 10 cowboys moved their horses towards cover. Adams dismounted and led his chestnut mare into a dry gully with Tomahawk at his side. They tethered their reins to a broad tree stump before moving up the steep crumbling slope until they were lying in brittle long grass. In total contrast to the heavily armed men moving around the high embankments, the two cowboys noticed a number of bedraggled men working at the very base of the timber dam.

'What you reckon them fellas is doing, Gene?' Tomahawk asked as he aimed a thin digit down at the filthy bunch.

'They are looking for something,' Adams replied.

'They sure don't look very well. Kinda liverish, if you ask me, Gene.'

Adams looked at his pal. 'They are Chinese, you old fool.'

'Chinese? What they doing here?' Tomahawk's eyes screwed up tightly as he tried to gain a better view.

'Beats me. Why would Johnson need a bunch of Chinese to wallow around at the base of his dam?' Adams shook his head as yet another question was added to the unanswered itinerary. Then he noticed one of the riflemen using the length of his Winchester to beat one of the thin Chinese into continuing his search.

'Them yellow varmints ain't there through choice, Gene.' Tomahawk nudged his partner. 'I think they is slaves.'

'I guess you might be right, old timer.' Adams gazed across the wide landscape taking everything in and trying to memorize it all. There were too many men with far too many guns for his liking. Riflemen who seemed uneasy and restless as they stood upon the opposite banks of the great chasm just waiting for something to fire at. Occasionally they would just fire down at the cracked mud itself as if practising terrifying the be-draggled Orientals.

'Rufas Johnson has got himself an army, Gene,' Tomahawk said woefully.

'Right enough, old timer. An army of gunmen and an army of slaves,' agreed Adams trying to count the men who protected the dam from those who would destroy it and return normality back to the parched lands of Sanora.

'What you figuring on doing?' Tomahawk ran a thumbnail along the honed edge of his hatchet blade as he studied the dam weeping as the swollen lake beyond tried desperately to breach the massive obstruction.

'Nothing right now, old timer.' Adams bit his lip. 'We better get back to Bessie's place. This is gonna take a bit of figuring. Too much figuring to be rushed.'

'We ain't gonna do nothing?' Tomahawk followed the silver-haired man down the slope back to their mounts.

'Right now we gotta tell the women about the funeral.' Adams untied his reins from around the tree stump before mounting once more.

'I forgot about that.'

'This ain't a place to visit during the day, Tomahawk.' The eyes of the mature rancher seemed alert to the many lethal weapons a mere quarter mile off. Alert to the fact a carbine had the range to shoot them out of their saddles before they even heard the shot. 'This is a place which requires visiting after sunset.'

Tomahawk climbed into his saddle and dragged the horse full around until he was level with his friend.

'I think I understand.' Tomahawk tapped his legs against the sides of his quarter horse and followed his companion. 'I reckon we will need to bring all our hands down from the Bar 10 to help us with this problem.'

Adams shook his head at the idea. He knew the odds were stacked against them but something inside the white-haired rancher still relished such problems. He had built the Bar 10 into one of the biggest ranches in Texas by sheer grit and defiance. He had defied the Indians and all those who could only see the hardships and none of the benefits of creating such an empire in the then untamed wilderness. Now four decades later he faced an even less certain future. Not on his own land, but out in the parched dying plains of another man's macabre ambitions. There were too many unanswered questions surrounding Rufas Johnson. He was not creating something good like the Bar 10, but destroying everything in order to achieve a secret goal. Adams vowed to discover the reason.

'Nope. Our boys will stay up on the Bar 10 tending the longhorns. I ain't gonna start no range war,' Gene Adams said in a masterful voice as he steered his chestnut close to the ragged embankment of brush.

'But, Gene?'

'We can handle this Johnson character and his men, Tomahawk.'

'Sure we can,' Tomahawk gulped. 'After all, there are three of us.'

TWELVE

During the hours of darkness as the two Ward women slept, Gene Adams and his two Bar 10 rannies kept vigil. They had placed torches around the fence poles to give them light and to deter attackers from trying to repeat the previous evening's bloodbath. Johnny had found a nice soft spot up in the hay loft of the stables where he waited with his two six-guns fully loaded and a carbine across his lap. If anyone ventured towards the Ward ranch he would be first to spot them.

Old Tomahawk sat wrapped in an Indian blanket behind an upturned water barrel with his Colt in one hand and his razor-sharp hatchet in the other.

Gene Adams moved in and out of the darkened house every half hour or so with canteens filled with hot sweet coffee to keep his men alert.

For the first three hours nothing stirred out on the poor parched land but then as midnight approached, the sound of a rider seemed to echo about the buildings.

Adams ran past Tomahawk to the corral and ducked through the poles until he was standing directly below Johnny's vantage point.

'What can you see, Johnny?' Adams yelled.

Johnny stood and gazed out at the flat black plain until he spotted the rider illuminated by their blazing torches.

'It's that critter on the roan, Gene.'

Adams climbed the poles until he could see beyond the courtyard and squinted.

'It is him.'

'He's heading this way,' Johnny added.

'Tomahawk?' Adams called out to his old friend peering from behind the barrel as he jumped back down onto the hard ground.

'What?' the old timer replied.

'It's the Red Roan Rider. Don't fire.' Gene

Adams pulled his hat brim down as he stood watching the approaching rider tearing across the dry plain.

'What in tarnation does he want?' The old man moved through the cold night air beneath his blanket and only paused when he was beside the tall Adams.

Adams gritted his teeth. 'I reckon you'll be able to ask him yourself shortly.'

The masked rider seemed either unafraid of the three gun-toting men or simply in too much of a hurry to give them a second thought as he thundered into the courtyard. Reining in his magnificent stallion he sat motionless for a moment until Gene Adams stepped towards him. Only then did he raise a hand as if gesturing for the white-haired man to stop.

'What's wrong, stranger?' Adams asked frowning.

The rider pointed at Adams and then up at Johnny Puma who was perched high in the open hay loft window.

'You want me and Johnny?'

The masked rider nodded and then gestured with his hands for them to get their mounts and follow him.

'You want me and Johnny to come with you?' Adams rubbed the back of his neck. Trying to read another man's mind did not come naturally to the rancher yet he knew why silence filled the cold night air. The rider upon the roan must be someone they had already encountered or would soon meet. Someone whose voice would betray his identity.

The rider nodded again as he wrestled with his reins atop the magnificent stallion.

'What about me, Gene?' Tomahawk asked. 'I oughta be there with you in case you gets yourself dry-gulched.'

Adams turned towards the old man.

'You stay here and make sure nobody hurts them ladies. Me and the young'un can handle this.'

Johnny slid down the rope hanging from a pulley with his rifle tucked through his belt. As his Cuban heels hit the dry ground he moved like the big cat he had been named after to Gene Adams's side.

'We gonna go with this fella, Gene?'

Adams nodded.

'Saddle my chestnut and your pinto. We're gonna go for a ride with the masked stranger.'

'But why, Gene?' Johnny stood staring up at the man in crimson with more than a little doubt filling his breast.

'Because I've got me a hankering to know what this masked rider is so darned fired up about,' Adams replied. 'Saddle the horses, son. I'll take care of you.'

As the youthful Johnny Puma headed towards the stable he mumbled under his breath.

'I'll look after Johnny and I'm sure Bessie will look after you, old timer.' Adams grinned at the blanket standing next to him. A blanket with a beard protruding from out of it.

THIRTEEN

It stood out like a beacon against the backdrop of stars pinned to the black night sky. The old whitewashed Spanish mission had been standing on the same tranquil spot for nearly a hundred and fifty years, unabashed by time nor politics. Unaffected by anything the outside world could conceive until Johnson had constructed his dam. Now even here the once sweet grass was dying and God's missionaries could no longer turn a blind eye. Gene Adams and Johnny had followed the red roan through the winding trails for over an hour before reaching this sacred place. Adams respectfully removed his dark Stetson when they approached. It had been some time since he was last this close to such a structure and the silver-haired man felt uneasy.

The Red Roan Rider dismounted and tied his reins to a long hitching rail and waited for the Bar 10 men. Johnny Puma had never seen a mission with a bell tower before and was in awe of its presence here in the heart of the parched wilderness.

'Why did you bring us here, stranger?' Johnny asked as he stood beside his pony tying the long leather reins tightly to the pole as Adams stepped down from his chestnut mare beside him.

'Easy, Johnny.' Adams said patting the younger man's arm. 'I'm sure our friend will enlighten us when he's a mind to.'

The hooded man removed his hat and moved to the large heavy doors silently. He turned the massive brass ring handle and pushed it open.

'Come in.'

Adams looked at Johnny before returning his amazed stare at the masked man.

'So you can talk after all,' Adams remarked as he attempted vainly to recognize the voice by so few words. It was a deep voice which hinted of many accents without revealing any.

The Red Roan Rider nodded and walked into the mission where a dozen candles burned across the altar around a three foot tall silver cross encrusted with gems. Light danced around the interior of the holy place as if greeting its visitors.

Adams stood beside the man who seemed totally preoccupied by something they could not imagine. Johnny Puma found himself removing his own Stetson without knowing why as he edged his way into the sacrosanct place. The air within the small chapel had the scent of something neither of the Bar 10 men had ever experienced before. It seemed to relax their nerves as they followed the masked stranger between the pews toward a side door which led deeper into the building.

'Where we going, Gene?' Johnny asked as he trailed the two men.

Adams gazed back at his young friend and placed a finger to his lips as if gesturing for silence whilst he thought about their situation.

The masked man hesitated at the door and tapped it lightly with his gloved knuckles. Then they heard a faint voice from within bidding them entry.

Adams and Johnny walked slowly behind the man in crimson into the room illuminated by two large candles set upon a square wooden table. At the table a solitary Jesuit priest sat before a massive opened bible. The priest looked directly at the three men and smiled as he gestured to the vacant chairs around the table.

'Welcome, my friends.'

Adams placed his hat on the table and drew up a chair closest to the man in his simple robes. Robes that could not disguise his Latin origins.

'Thank you kindly, Father. My name's Adams.'

The priest nodded knowingly as he watched all three men sitting down before him.

'I know who you and your friend are, Gene Adams.'

Adams's eyes flashed across at Johnny before looking back at the face of the holy man.

'You do?'

'My friend here has told me about you and your companions and of your mission.' The priest was smiling at the hooded man who sat silently at the end of the table. 'My name is Father Gonzales and this is the mission of St Mary.'

'Why have you brought us here, Father Gonzales?' Adams asked as he tried to allow himself to relax whilst every instinct in his body warned him to be on his guard. The past couple of days had caused him to doubt even this frail religious man.

'I asked my masked friend to bring you to my mission because you came here to help your friend Brook Ward.' Father Gonzales sighed. 'I knew you were probably the only men within a hundred miles of St Mary's mission that I could totally trust.'

'Trust?' Adams chewed on the word thoughtfully.

'Si, my friend. Trust,' the priest repeated.

'You talk about trust but why does your friend wear a mask like an outlaw, Father?' Johnny asked as he stared across at the quiet hooded man. 'He don't trust us with knowing who he is.'

Gonzales looked at the young Bar 10 cowboy and patted his hand knowingly. 'He is a good man who has to keep his identity secret because if it were known who he was, death would visit his family.'

'Death?' Adams sat upright.

'There are evil forces at work in and around Sanora, Gene Adams.' The priest shook his head in frustration. 'I cannot tell you how evil. This is one truth which you already have tasted at first hand. My masked friend is probably the bravest man I have ever known for he alone has faced our enemies. Until you came to help a friend with no thought to your own safety. I trust you and your friends, Gene Adams.'

'We've had a taste of your enemy's venom ourselves, Father Gonzales,' Adams agreed.

'Is Rufas Johnson behind all the killings and mayhem?' Johnny asked staring from the Red Roan Rider to the holy man.

'He is,' the Red Roan Rider responded quietly disguising his voice carefully.

'Me and my pal Tomahawk seen the dam he has built across the river. He has Chinese slaves digging there. Why?' Adams's tone was getting more urgent.

Father Gonzales placed both his wrinkled hands upon the book before him and lowered his head for a brief moment as if seeking strength in prayer.

'I know the secret which has caused so much pain and death in my parish,' the father said softly. 'A secret bathed in blood from long ago. A secret which somehow Rufas Johnson discovered, bringing him here.'

'Secret? What kinda secret?' Johnny Puma rested his elbows on the thick oak surface of the table as he found himself drawn to the priest.

Adams raised a thoughtful eyebrow. 'I'm real curious, Father Gonzales. What do you mean exactly when you say "secret"?'

The wise priest sat back in his chair and rested his spine against the wooden frame. Glaring into the flickering flame of the nearest candle he began to tell his audience of a story which would chill each and every one of them as it slowly unfolded from his thin lined lips.

'This is a story which you may dismiss as mere legend but I swear on this holy book, every word I say is the utter truth.'

Gene Adams could not take his eyes from the priest.

'Go on, Father. Maybe if you can throw some light onto this mystery, I might have some idea what to do.'

Father Gonzales crossed himself and smiled into the flame of the candle and continued. 'It all began a hundred and fifty years ago when the first foundations of St Mary's Mission were being laid into this once fertile soil beneath our feet. It was a time long before men such as yourselves rode this land we now call Texas. A time when missions were being built in every remote corner of the Americas in order to try and bring Christianity to its native people.

'Whilst priests such as myself risked their lives in these untamed lands with only their faith as protection, a very different sort of conversion was taking place elsewhere along America's endless coastline. For over a century the Spanish had been stripping the wealth from these lands and taking it back to the Old World. For the most part they had little trouble but then the tide began to turn.

'You see, my friends, this was a time when pirates plied their evil trade around the Indies. A time when Spanish galleons sailed swollen with plunder. They had destroyed countless Indian civilizations and looted their wealth, hiding behind the guise of Christianity versus the heathen, using cannons against bows and arrows in order to proclaim this land for God. But they had not bargained for the pirates. Ship after ship, decade after decade the Spanish left the shores of the Americas filled with the gold and precious jewels stolen from the Inca and other civilizations. Golden works of art were smelted into bullion bars to be taken back to the Old World. Jewels of every kind were ripped from the necks of the natives and filled into chests before being loaded onto the Spanish ships. Hundreds maybe even thousands of ships took the wealth of this land back to Spain before the pirates closed in and started to attack the slow, heavily laden, vessels burdened with treasure. Then there were the pirates, many of whom were in fact acting for the English monarchy trying to divert the treasures into their own hands. Other pirates worked purely for self-gain and had smaller faster vessels capable of moving in close and beneath the cannons of the tall galleons. They would row these smaller vessels up behind the massive galleons and agile sailors would jam the rudders so the bigger ship could not be steered. When the Spanish found their ship was helpless they would panic. Then the pirates would storm up over the vessel's walls and fight to the death until they had what they wanted: the treasure. After they had completed their task many pirates would take their plunder to secret places to share out the booty in prearranged percentages. Places such as Sanora.'

Adams's face seemed to come to life as he began to see the story in his mind's eye coming to life. 'Sanora? I'm beginning to understand.'

Father Gonzales bowed his head. 'Si, my friend. There was one such pirate who found in the deep waters of the mouth of the Nueces River, a sanctuary for his trim ship. His name was Henry Black and he had a hundred or more men under his command. He sailed into the natural bay where the town of Sanora now stands and weighed anchor between his murderous raids. Here his men would carefully maintain his ship's seaworthy state by careening her. This was a difficult task where they would have to put the ship upon its side and scrape all the barnacles and weed from its wooden underbelly. Weeds slowed down a ship and the pirates required speed for their very survival. For many years Henry Black brought his victorious treasure here to spend in the town which grew around the bay. This little mission was partly funded by that wealth.'

'A pirate building a mission?' Johnny gasped.

'Black was no evil bloodthirsty cut-throat like many of his profession but a man who in his own way simply tried to restore the balance which had so long been tipped in Spain's favour. A sort of Robin Hood, if you like.' Father Gonzales gazed at the three men around the table.

'He built this mission?' Gene Adams repeated Johnny's question.

'This and many other things. Black created Sanora. A church is a very good thing to keep one's men in check. He knew he had to keep these men from becoming animals and sometimes praying to a greater Being can make even the most ruthless soul realize his own limitations. He also built many taverns.' Father Gonzales' eyes began to twinkle as a wry smile covered his lips.

Adams nodded.

'I guess you're saying this Henry Black was in fact trying to give something back to the people who had been so brutally robbed.'

'Si, Gene Adams,' the priest sighed.

'Who the heck was this Robin Hood character, Gene?' Johnny asked scratching his head.

'Just a fella from the east, Johnny,' Adams replied.

Gonzales continued. 'Then, one day, Black is said to have taken on one fateful Spanish galleon too many. He sailed with his crew out into the Gulf and managed to strike with his usual speed and expertise. Unfortunately, his own ship was severely damaged and caught fire, but he and his men boarded the galleon which he had holed along the waterline. His hundred heavily armed men fought the Spanish soldiers on the decks of the galleon until the ship was theirs. Realizing the galleon was taking on water, Black brought the ship back here in order to beach her in shallow water up river where his men could make repairs; however, the ship was laden with so much gold it began to sink much faster than Black had anticipated. Black's mastery of seamanship managed to bring the huge vessel up into the Nueces River but before he was able to sail up into shallow water, it finally went down with its entire treasure still in its holds.'

Adams began to smile across at his young friend.

'That's what Johnson has them Chinese digging for, Johnny.'

'Treasure?'

'Yep. Treasure.' Adams ran his fingers over his face. 'Rufas Johnson somehow managed to find out about the ship sinking with its belly full of gold bullion and precious gems and decided to build himself a dam to drain the water from out of the river slowly.'

'Exactly.' The Red Roan Rider said, 'Johnson has no pity on the people and creatures dying as a consequence of the water being starved from here, only his own greed. His single-minded ambition to find the treasure buried under a hundred and fifty years of mud has blurred his humanity.'

'I guess the phoney Indian attacks were just a crude way of speeding up folks into quitting Sanora,' Adams snarled quietly.

'Si, Gene Adams.' Father Gonzales ran the palms of his hands over the pages of his bible as he stared at the white-haired rancher beside him.

'What happened to Henry Black and his crew, Father?'

'After the galleon sank, Black and his men turned their backs upon piracy and used their remaining wealth to help the people of this land. Black became a respected citizen of Sanora.' Father Gonzales got to his feet and moved around the table slowly.

'You said this story was based on fact?' Adams studied the priest as he hesitated behind the chair where the hooded man was seated.

'It is all written down in the history of St Mary's Mission for all to read.' Gonzales sighed. 'All who can read Latin, that is.'

'What connection has our Red Roan Rider friend here have to all of this, sir?' Johnny Puma asked.

Placing his hands upon the shoulders of the man clad entirely in crimson, the priest spoke softly.

'This is the descendant of Henry Black.'

'So your name's Black, huh?' Johnny smiled at the hooded man.

'Nope. My name ain't Black,' the masked man chuckled.

'Now we must try and create a plan, my friends,' Father Gonzales said as he entered the chapel with the three men following him.

'Oh, I've already figured out what I've gotta do, Father,' Adams said as his words echoed around the interior of the mission.

'I do not wish to see a man such as yourself breaking the law,' Father Gonzales frowned.

'Gene never breaks the law, sir,' Johnny chipped in.

'But I have been known to bend it a tad...' Adams nodded to himself.

FOURTEEN

The morning wind swept across the dusty graveyard as Brook Ward's crude wooden coffin was carefully lowered by his friends and the undertaker into the six-foot deep chasm. The ground was baked so hard it had taken pickaxes to break through its solid crust. Even at the required depth, there was still no moisture. The small hundred-foot-square graveyard was hot as it stood on a slight rise at the edge of Sanora. The breeze did not cool any of the assembled mourners as it blew the fine granules of dust into their eyes. Black clothing appeared grey, making a mockery of the respectful occasion. People stood trying to pay their last respects whilst nature continued to display its anger at being maimed so mercilessly.

Gene Adams looked around the faces of the gathering as the elderly priest from St Mary's Mission read the funeral service. Most were faces of people he had not seen before. Hard weathered faces, thin from lack of water and good food. These were what was left of Sanora's once healthy population, he mused. These people were all who remained of pirate captain Henry Black and his crew's descendants. A bunch of broken souls. Paying his last respects, Sheriff Tiberius Fox stood silently with his head lowered, flanked by his two deputies, his red mane of hair flapping angrily in the cutting morning breeze. A breeze which could take the shine off the star he so proudly wore upon his silk vest beneath his long dark tail-coat. Jim Jones eyed the small crowd with a blank emotionless expression whilst deputy Dick Smith appeared less than happy to be so close to death.

Adams knew this was an occasion charged with a multitude of subdued hostilities. Each and every one of the men, women and children standing listening to the words being delivered by Father Gonzales was at breaking point. Each and every face displayed the same expression. It was the look of revenge.

Tomahawk seemed unusually quiet as he stared at the open hole and the coffin. The old timer seldom showed any signs of emotion but today he was visibly upset. When you reached Tomahawk's age, whatever it was, you could only lose so many friends before they were all gone.

Anita Ward leaned heavily upon Johnny's broad frame as she wept continually into her small lace handkerchief. Adams wondered if any of these people might be the hooded man who had guided Johnny and himself to and from the old mission of St Mary's during the hours of darkness. If he was here, Adams could not identify him. There were at least four men standing around the grave who matched the height of the Red Roan Rider. Any of whom might have just cause to rebel against a tyrant like Johnson.

As Father Gonzales finished reading the funeral service the small crowd of Sanora's remaining citizens heard the rumble of riders heading in their direction at speed. At first it sounded like distant thunder then it became obvious – it was hooves thundering across the hard dead soil.

Gene Adams's eyes were the first to spot the dust rising to the north as he stood beside his friend's widow comforting her with his gloved left hand. Carefully he shielded his hand from view with the large black ten gallon hat as his right thumb flicked off the safety loop from the gold-plated Colt hanging on his right hip. Slipping his index finger into the trigger guard of the holstered weapon he rested the palm of his hand upon the grip and waited.

'Riders, Gene,' Tomahawk said moving beside the tall rancher and pointing at the dust.

'I saw it a while back. Keep your hand on that old hatchet of yours, old timer,' Adams ordered through gritted teeth as he watched the dust rising into the morning sky. 'I might need you to split a skull with that old relic.'

'I'm ready, Gene. I'm real ready.' Tomahawk tried vainly to force his beard down with his hand but it returned to its usual place and jutted out in the direction of the approaching riders.

Johnny Puma strode to the side of his two Bar 10 comrades and pushed the still sobbing Anita Ward behind the tall frame of Adams protectively.

"Them riders are coming in darn fast, Gene.'

'They ain't all riders, Johnny,' Adams noted as he clearly saw a black sealed carriage at the heart of the dozen or more horses. 'If my instincts are correct, we are gonna meet the infamous Rufas Johnson.'

'About time,' Tomahawk spat.

'It sure is,' Johnny agreed.

The dust which followed the riders reining in at the gate of the cemetery swept over the mourners as Adams led his men and the entire population of Sanora down from the rise.

Stepping out of the carriage drawn by a matched pair of geldings, Rufas Johnson stood holding a large bandanna to his face as if unwilling to choke on the dust he had created like everyone else. He cut a strange figure. His girth so wide in its circumference it seemed almost unreal. It was clear by his appearance he, unlike the citizens of Sanora and its outlying farms and ranches, was neither hungry nor having to ration his water. The dozen gunhands had dismounted and surrounded their leader before Adams and his followers had reached the gate.

'You Rufas Johnson?' Adams asked still shielding his right hand gun with his large Stetson.

Tiberius Fox strolled next to Adams and glanced at the rancher.

'This is Rufas Johnson, Adams.'

Johnson waved his bandanna as he stepped forward flanked by his heavily armed men.

'I am indeed Rufas Johnson. Who are you?'

'They call me Adams,' the Bar 10 man said through teeth firmly gritted together.

Johnson shrugged.

'If your name is supposed to mean something it doesn't.'

Johnson's top gun, Burl Nunn, edged closer to his boss, leaning over and whispering something into the man's ear. As he spoke, Johnson's expression altered.

'Gene Adams of the Bar 10?' the rotund man asked in a low shallow tone.

Adams nodded slowly, 'Yep.'

'You're an awful long way from home, Adams.'

'I'd ride a thousand miles to help a pal, Johnson,' Adams spoke through his gritted teeth.

'Help a pal? Who have you come to help exactly?' Johnson's face was pale and devoid of any hint it had ever spent more than the briefest time out in the Texan climate.

Adams stepped forward but immediately

found six of Johnson's men standing between himself and his verbal target.

'Easy, boys!' Sheriff Fox said loudly waving at both sides of the two very different groups. 'I want you all to simmer down a little. Tempers are frayed and it's hot and windy and we've all eaten too much dust this morning.'

'I hear you, Fox. But do they?' Adams's eyes were locked onto those of Burl Nunn's as they stood toe to toe. Neither man spoke as they just glared into each other's souls seeking but not finding any weaknesses.

Tiberius Fox forced the two big men apart and then moved towards the figure of Johnson.

'You ain't the most popular critter in these parts, Mister Johnson,' Fox said over the shoulders of the fat man's guards.

'I have come here on business, sheriff.' Johnson tapped his men to part and allow the lawman to approach. 'Can you object to my spending money in your pathetic town? I have come to this terrible little place in order to buy provisions.'

'I ain't paid to object to anything. I'm paid to try and keep the peace. A peace which is mighty hard to keep with your actions of late.' Fox chewed on his own spit as he spoke trying not to let fly and cover the man he detested in spittle. 'If you wanna spend your money, I'll see you do so unharmed.'

'What have I done? I've done nothing to warrant anyone harming me, have I?' Johnson made a face which pleaded to be punched and would have been, if any of the mourners could have managed to get close enough.

'Building a dam and cutting off the water from Sanora is an act against God and His people, my son,' Father Gonzales said loudly as he joined the main group of mourning townspeople.

'What I do on my land is my business,' Johnson replied from behind Nunn's protective shoulder.

'God will punish you!' the priest added forcefully.

'Then I shall answer to Him, not any of you,' Johnson added.

The crowd seemed restless as it moved behind the Bar 10 men who stood shoulder to shoulder facing the gunmen and their leader.

'This is a sad day for us,' Adams interrupted. 'We just buried a man who was killed by Indians but there ain't no Indians, are there? Just a bunch of white men wearing wigs and using bows and arrows.'

'Am I supposed to know what you're driving at, Adams?' the fat man snorted.

'We both know the answer to that, Johnson. Like I said, this is a sad occasion as most funerals are,' Gene Adams replied.

'A funeral is never a joyous occasion, Adams.' Johnson smirked trying to ignore the suggestion that he knew more about the phoney Indians than he would care to admit. Confident in the knowledge it was impossible to prove he had any connection with the brutal death of Brook Ward.

'I reckon your funeral might cause a few

folks to feel a tad happier,' Adams grinned. 'I figure, I for one would be right joyous at that service, Johnson.'

'That is an outrageous statement!' Rufas Johnson boomed as he suddenly felt the hatred of those who looked at him.

Fox managed to move the dozen heavily armed men and Johnson down towards the town with the help of his two deputies whilst Gene Adams stood beside Bessie Ward watching.

'So that's Johnson,' she said dabbing her eyes with a small lace handkerchief. 'I thought he'd be bigger.'

'He casts a big enough shadow, old girl,' Adams sighed. 'Big enough to spread its darkness over an entire community.'

FIFTEEN

'I want Gene Adams dead before sun up, Burl,' Rufas Johnson snarled as he poured himself another tall brandy from the crystal decanter within his study. 'Dead. Do you understand?'

Nunn moved to the side of his employer and toyed with his gun as he lifted up a bottle of whiskey and drank from the neck of the black glass bottle. The sun still raged outside the massive building bringing its venom to those who dwelt on the south of this place.

'And his men. And those damn women.' Johnson paced up and down the long room rotating the amber liquid in his glass. 'All of them dead. Take a dozen men and kill them all. Now.'

'You is forgetting a couple of things, boss,'

Nunn said as he wiped the whiskey from his chin onto his sleeve.

Johnson paused.

'What am I forgetting? I remember that cowboy insulting me as if he were better than me.'

'We can't use the Indian ploy again. They're wise to that.'

'So? Just send some men in and kill them all.' Johnson's facial colour turned red as he bristled with anger.

Nunn took another mouthful of whiskey and swallowed hard before continuing. 'Then the law will have no option but to come here and lay the blame at your feet. Sheriff Fox could justify sending for the Texas Rangers.'

'Why? Do you think I have only the gunmen on my pay-roll in Texas?' Johnson drank the warm liquid down as he had done several thousand times previously over the past few decades. 'How could they prove they are my men, Burl?'

'I reckon them folks wouldn't need proof.'

Nunn stared at the bottle as he spoke. 'They is damn angry and when folks get angry enough they fight back. They ain't gonna worry about proving nothing. They'll just come in shooting.'

'And we'll kill them all. We have more men here than there are in the rest of this damn county.' Johnson laughed loudly as he staggered back to the decanter. 'Men with guns. The best guns with the best ammunition and, unlike the folks out there, they are paid to kill.'

'We have not got so many men we can afford to risk losing any more of them.' Nunn put the bottle to his mouth and poured the burning rotgut down his throat once more.

Johnson turned to the tall gunslinger and stared.

'I want Adams dead. Tonight.'

'We got four men dead and wounded. I have six men guarding the dam and the coolies. I got only a dozen here right now able to fight.' Burl Nunn placed the bottle down and walked to the large window which looked out at the lush courtyard. 'I take a dozen men from here and you have nobody left to defend you and this place.'

'Hire more men, Burl,' Johnson ranted.

'It takes time to hire men. I'd have to ride to Laredo in order to find the sort we want.' Nunn rested a hand upon the white wooden surround of the window and looked across the fertile grounds. Once the whole of Sanora had looked as green and lush until they had arrived.

'How long would it take?'

'At least two weeks. Maybe even longer,' Nunn replied.

Johnson smashed a plump right fist into the palm of his left hand angrily.

'But we have to kill Adams. He's trouble.'

Nunn shrugged and stared back over his wide shoulder straight into the face of his inebriated employer.

'I don't recommend stirring up any more trouble with them Bar 10 hombres, boss.'

Rufas Johnson paced around the room

sipping at his brandy trying to think above his indignation.

'There are a dozen men around the house?'

'Roughly,' Nunn said.

Johnson gave a massive sigh. 'Choose the six best gunmen from the sentries and send them back to the Ward place. Adams ought to be back there before nightfall. Tell them I'll give each man a hundred dollar bonus if they bring back Adams's scalp.'

'We ought to wait for him to strike here. Then he'll be trespassing and we'll have to kill him.' Nunn gave a slight chuckle. 'It would be legal and nobody could say anything to the contrary.'

Johnson laughed for the first time since he had returned from Sanora. 'You can choose the six men, Burl. That's an order.'

Nunn did not bother to try and deter the exasperated Rufas Johnson any further. He strode from the large house and was gone for nearly thirty minutes. As Johnson leaned against the huge window he watched as the half dozen riders thundered away from his ranch and a solemn faced Burl Nunn marched back from the stables and into the house. The gunslinger said nothing as he picked up the whiskey bottle again and strode back to the side of his soft-skinned employer.

'It's done,' Nunn snapped with more than a hint of disapproval in his voice.

'Tonight I'll have the scalp of that white-haired bastard hanging over my door, Burl,' Johnson laughed with a confidence not customary for him.

'I've told the remaining hands to spread out and keep their wits about them, boss,' Nunn said fearing he had now helped the large girthed man make yet another false move. A move which might just bring the Bar 10 cowboys to this place.

Staring over the length of the black glass bottle as he sucked its venomous liquid into his dry mouth, Burl Nunn suddenly spotted something which made him stand upright and call to his employer who had started to wander back to the drinks table for yet another refill.

'Frankie is coming in from the dam, boss. He's riding damn hard.'

'Frankie?' Johnson rushed to the side of his top gunslinger and looked out through the window at the approaching horseman.

'He looks kinda excited, boss,' Nunn noted.

'At last. At last. Do you think…?'

Nunn moved from the window to the large wooden doors with his round bellied employer on his heels. Rushing out onto the porch just as the rider drew in his reins and leapt from the horse the two men could see the excited expression carved across the guard's features.

'We found something, boss,' the bedraggled gunman known simply as Frankie said.

'What they find?' Burl Nunn grabbed at the younger man's sleeve and steadied him.

'A box!' Frankie exclaimed loudly.

Nunn grabbed the young man's face and

pulled it to him. 'A wooden chest?'

'Yep. A real old wooden chest, Burl,' the guard confirmed gleefully.

Nunn turned to the red-eyed Johnson and grinned wider than he had ever grinned in his entire life before.

'Reckon you was right, boss. That old map of yours must have been the genuine article.'

'Finally.' Johnson rested a hand upon the wooden upright and tried to regain his wind. 'I knew I was right. Didn't I always say that map was real, Burl?'

'You sure did.' Burl Nunn eagerly grabbed the reins from Frankie's grasp and mounted the listless animal before dragging the creature full circle.

'Frankie. Get Mister Johnson's carriage.'

'Where are you going, Burl?' Rufas Johnson asked his top gunhand.

'I'm gonna take me a look at what them boys have dug outta the mud, boss.' Nunn spurred the creature and galloped in the direction of the distant dam.

Johnson stepped down from the porch and pushed the confused figure of Frankie hard in the direction of the stables.

'You heard him. Get my carriage. Now!' Johnson commanded as he began to regret his action at sending half his able-bodied guards off on a mission which just might backfire. 'Round up the sentries as well, Frankie. We are all going down to the dam.'

Within the hour Johnson had drawn every one of his men from their various posts and sent them down into the mud below the dam, to assist the painfully frail Chinese in retrieving one wooden chest after another. By the time the sun was beginning to set and the light starting to fail, the two dozen men – including the Chinese – had managed to drag five huge locked wooden chests up the steep embankment away from their hundred and fifty year old burial place.

At first the rotund man had thought the chests might be rotten but somehow the mud's strange properties had preserved the wooden creations perfectly. Only the locks and hinges were rusted and resisted several attempts by Nunn to break open the heavy reinforced treasure boxes.

Rufas Johnson forced his way through the unrecognizable figures and fell onto his knees beside one of the chests. The men watched dumb struck as he stroked the box in an almost feverish manner, as if it were a female he had long desired.

Nunn hovered over his boss and stared around the mud covered faces before looking down at the man.

'We'd better call it a day, boss.'

'No, no. Send them down to get more. There must be dozens more chests waiting to be discovered!' Johnson blurted.

'It's too dark, boss.' Nunn rubbed the palms of his hands on the seat of his jeans and nodded at the men to head back to their quarters. Slowly the men dragged their weary bones away from the scene.

Johnson hauled himself back onto his feet and called at his men loudly. 'Load these chests onto the buckboards, boys.'

The men paused and looked to Nunn, who nodded, before obeying the orders of the man who paid their wages.

Johnson suddenly wondered why the guards seemed to double-check his commands with Burl Nunn before responding.

'Why did they wait for you to agree with my orders before obeying, Burl?'

'They're tired, boss. These men have been using muscles and they ain't paid to do nothing except use their weapons,' Nunn replied as he watched the sun disappearing below the horizon.

'Tomorrow we shall retrieve the rest of the treasure.'

'How many more chests are there?'

'At least another hundred.'

Nunn made an expression which was masked by the darkening sky and fading light. For the first time since he had taken Johnson's blood money, he wondered whether they actually needed him any longer.

'Come on, boss. We'll get back to the house and start trying to bust these chests apart,' the gunslinger said as he followed the portly man towards the waiting carriage and the horses. 'I've a feeling the contents are something beyond imagination.'

Johnson glared at the tall man beside him thoughtfully.

'Nothing is beyond my imagination, Burl. Remember that.'

SIXTEEN

There seemed little logic in it but Gene Lon Adams had had his belly-full of logic. Now it was time to act. Not for himself but for the people of Sanora plus Bessie Ward and her daughter. After the funeral, he had made the two unwilling females remain in the town whilst he and his two trusty companions rode back to the small Ward spread. This time they had a pack mule in tow – a mule laden down with dynamite sticks and fuses. Adams had never been the sort to flaunt the law but in his heart he was not breaking anything anywhere near the law as he knew it. He had seen the town and its people slowly dying before his very eyes over the past couple of days and he knew somebody had to act now. Sanora needed water and Gene Adams was going to get it for them, no matter what it might cost him personally.

The tall chestnut mare cantered along the trail of dust before the black quarter horse and the pinto pony. The three riders were in no hurry. They had an entire night to complete their mission and the new moon seemed to be on their side as it illuminated their path back to the ranch Brook Ward had built. All three riders wondered if the farmhouse would still be standing after their brief absence. Johnson and his henchmen might have detoured there and finished the deed they had attempted to start two nights earlier. The ride was longer than usual, and they could have moved faster had they not been leading the mule with its deadly cargo strapped to its ornery spine.

Then, as they turned their mounts up the trail towards the fenced courtyard towards the farmhouse, the air lit up with a dozen blazing shafts of murderous red tapers. The noise was deafening as rifle fire echoed about the small troop. Gene Adams desperately tried to control his terrified mare as one of the bullets crashed into the right-hand side of his saddle's fork just between the rigging straps and forced the animal down onto the ground by its sheer power. Adams screamed in pain as the winded creature lay snorting across his trapped left leg.

Tomahawk slid from his horse and dragged the alarmed animal towards the cover of a ten foot high boulder. Screwing up his wrinkled eyes he attempted to work out what was happening to his younger friends amid the red streaks of deadly bullet traces which kept on coming. The edge of the boulder cracked as a half dozen rifle bullets tore into it cascading dust over the grim-faced old man. The black quarter horse reared in terror and rode off into the darkness.

'Gene's down, Johnny!' Tomahawk yelled as he saw the felled chestnut struggling on top of the helpless rancher.

Johnny Puma dismounted quickly and

slapped his pony away from the danger. It galloped from the blazing air which was filled with flashing streaks of death and the stinking scent of gunpowder.

Kneeling with both his guns drawn, the young cowboy watched as the pinto was followed by their pack mule before he began to fire his weapons in the various directions of the rifle blasts. After he had used up half his twelve chambers of cartridges, he raced across the flat ground and slid down beside Adams. Holstering both his weapons the youngster tried to drag the big man away from the saddle but it had him pinned. Another flurry of bullets came at them. Most seemed aimed at Tomahawk who was stuck behind the boulder unable to move away. The cloudless sky and the bright new moon seemed to be upon the side of the bushwhackers as Johnny dragged the Winchester from its scabbard upon Adams's saddle.

'We got about five or six varmints trying to shoot us up, Gene,' Johnny announced as he cranked the rifle and fired angrily at the hidden sniper. 'I hate dry gulchers.'

'Easy, Johnny,' Adams gasped. 'Aim true boy. We ain't got enough ammunition to waste a single shell.'

The young cowboy took a deep lung of air and waited for the next volley of bullets to rain in upon them. When the first two flashes of light lit up the dark hiding places of two of their attackers, Johnny pushed the carbine lever down and then quickly back up before firing a carefully aimed shot. Even above the noise of the bullets, which were pouring in at the three men, his youthful ears heard the sound of a man falling. Faster than seemed humanly possible to the stricken Adams, the hands of Johnny Puma worked the rifle to claim another of their ruthless assailants.

Then Johnny's finger squeezed the trigger of the long rifle and a silence chilled his spine as the firing pin fell upon an empty chamber.

'Where's your Winchester shells, Gene?'

Johnny asked as he fell down beside the man.

'Under the horse in my saddlebags, Johnny,' Adams answered as he tried vainly to crawl away from the winded mare.

Johnny placed the carbine down and drew his Colts once more.

'This ain't good, Gene.'

'You winged two of them, Johnny,' the older man said as he patted the shaking shoulder of his pal.

'Two ain't all there is though.' The cowboy raised himself up slightly and fired at the shadows, knowing his bullets were falling short.

'Ain't got the range?' Adams asked.

'Nope. I ain't got anywhere close to the range, Gene.' Johnny rubbed the sweat from his brow as he lay beside the injured older man.

'I should have made sure my rifle was fully loaded.' Adams groaned as he put his Cuban heel on top of his saddle seat and tried to push himself clear of the mare again.

'Hell, Gene. I let my pinto run off before I had time to get my own rifle out of its sheath.' Johnny sucked in his breath as another volley of red streaks traced through the air a few feet above their heads.

Tomahawk fired his Colt as if trying frantically to draw their enemy's fire in his direction away from his trapped friends. It worked. Before he could pull his gun hammer back again, his shot was answered a dozen times over, lead ripping apart the side of the boulder as lethal rifle bullets acted like chisels upon the surface of the ancient stone. Dropping to his knees, the old timer coughed as he tried to clear his lungs and eyes of the burning stone fragments.

'Tarnation!' he shouted angrily at the ground.

'You OK, old timer?' Adams called across the distance between them.

'You bet, Gene,' Tomahawk lied spitting on his bandanna and rubbing the spit into his burning eyes.

'You hit?' Adams called out again.

'Nope. I'm just a tad dusty.'

Johnny emptied his spent shells and used up every remaining bullet from his belt in reloading the two Colts.

'We're in a little bit of trouble, Gene.'

'Reckon so, young 'un.' Adams fell onto his back exhausted at his wasted labours. His leg was still pinned down under his saddle and the full weight of his chestnut mare.

'You gotta plan yet?' Johnny moved close to the older greyer man.

'Wish I had.' Adams frowned.

'Not like you.'

'I don't think too clearly when I'm lying underneath a darn heavy horse, Johnny.' Adams tried to smile but the pain was too much.

'I got me a plan,' Johnny said.

'What kinda plan?' Gene Adams asked raising himself upon one elbow knowing the younger man only too well.

Johnny Puma grinned.

'I'll draw their fire.'

Gene Adams grabbed at Johnny's sleeve trying to stop him.

'Stay down.'

'I gotta get closer, Gene. It's the only way.'

SEVENTEEN

Suddenly the sound of a galloping horse out on the moonlit plain greeted the three trapped Bar 10 cowboys. Their attackers also heard the charging animal too, snorting as its hooves tore up the baked ground between them. For a split second, the firing paused as Rufas Johnson's hired killers realized someone was ignoring the ear-splitting noise emanating from their rifles and riding straight down their throats. Johnny knelt low staring out into the darkness at the trail he and his two friends had journeyed along only minutes earlier – a trail now being eaten up by the hooves of a familiar rider and mount.

The new moon cautiously gave the strange vision an almost ghost-like appearance as it thundered towards the Ward ranch. The hooded rider was standing in his stirrups allowing the red roan its full head, totally unafraid of the rifle shots which were now being directed only in his direction. Steering the huge stallion one way, then another, ever onward, the man behind the mask seemed oblivious to the bullets which raced out in his direction.

Before Johnny could speak, frantically the rifles had borne down upon the vision from their enemy's hiding places. Red streaks blazed out through the cold night air over the heads of Adams and Johnny Puma, filling the darkness with the sound and smell of death.

'Here comes that darn Red Roan Rider,' Johnny announced.

'Saving our bacon again,' Adams groaned as his weary eyes strained to focus upon the eerie image charging towards them.

Within fifty feet of the fence poles the masked rider dragged his reins hard to his left turning off the trail before disappearing beyond their line of sight to the west of the farmhouse. To the amazed onlookers it was as if the rider had vanished.

'Where the heck did he go?' Johnny grabbed at Adams's shoulder.

'How should I know?' Adams coughed. 'I bet you a week's wages he ain't gone far though.'

'I ain't taking no sucker bets, Gene.' Johnny leaned into the chestnut trying once more to encourage it to rise off the rancher's bruised leg.

'She'll get up when she's ready, Johnny. Not a minute before if she's anything like other females.' Adams shook his head trying to force the pain away in his beads of sweat.

'You should never have bought a mare, Gene,' Johnny gasped as he finally gave in his attempt to move the beast. 'Mares is finicky critters.'

'Where do you reckon that masked varmint went, boy?' There had been no time to answer the injured Bar 10 rancher's question when bullets flashed from beyond the farmhouse. A shriek echoed out around the courtyard as one of the bushwhackers fell out from his hiding place and tumbled across onto the moonlight bathed ground quite dead.

Johnny turned and stared over the saddle as he saw the three men sent by Rufas Johnson turning their attention and bullets upon their new target. The men fired desperately but the Red Roan Rider was no longer where their bullets were aimed. Johnny squinted as he saw the shape of the athletic man wearing the crimson clothes and hood leaping onto a fence pole and up to the farmhouse roof.

The hooded figure walked silently across the roof shingles, holding his .45 Peacemaker in his left hand whilst carrying his loose uncoiled bullwhip in the other. Pausing above the porch, the masked man flicked the long whip and caught one of Johnson's men cleanly around the neck. Twisting the whip until he had the vicious rawhide wrapped like a noose, the hooded man tightened his grip and lifted the kicking figure off his feet for a moment before allowing him to fall hard. The choking gunman felt the whip release before staggering around and firing up at the Red Roan Rider who loomed above him.

Another crack of the whip took the pistol from the man's grasp cleanly. Yelping as blood ran from his torn wrist, the gunman dashed towards the corral only to find the hooded man had managed to get there before him by leaping down off the corner of the single storey structure. Moving silently toward the sniper the hooded man seemed almost to shimmer in the faint eerie moonlight.

'What the hell are you?' the terrified killer shouted, throwing a fist at the strange hooded man's head desperately.

Without replying, the Red Roan Rider blocked the punch and cracked the skull of his opponent with the barrel of his gleaming Colt. Before the unconscious gunman had hit the ground, the hooded man had disappeared again into the shadows of the night seeking out the remaining men.

The two other bushwhackers stalked fearfully along the front of the farmhouse clutching their long Winchesters across their bellies gripped by a terror which was totally alien to them. They were seeking a phantom who seemed to be able to defy the laws of gravity. One minute he was on the ground whilst the next he was in the air above their heads.

Johnny Puma moved up from his cover behind the felled chestnut mare and raced along the dry baked ground towards the enemies who had lain in wait for him and his pals yet now appeared to have completely forgotten about them. Now they could think of only one target. A target who seemed more spirit than a living, breathing human being.

Keeping his head low, clutching both his guns, Johnny Puma aimed his boots directly at the farmhouse.

Suddenly one of the gunslingers spotted the figure of the youthful cowboy heading towards them in the moonlight.

'Look out!' he yelled as he cocked the carbine and raised it to his shoulder.

'What?' the other gunhand said spinning on his heels to face his comrade.

Before either could fire, Johnny squeezed both triggers and sent hot lead at the confused vermin, before falling onto his belly and rolling away from their blazing Winchesters.

As if from nowhere, the Red Roan Rider leapt down from the roof onto both the gunmen, sending them crushing into the solid ground.

Stunned, the two men wrestled with the Red Roan Rider until Johnny Puma sprang like a mountain lion into the heart of the action. Lifting one of the men off the ground, the handsome Bar 10 cowboy landed a gloved fist onto the tip of his jaw. The sound of the jaw cracking echoed around the structures as the gunman fell at his feet. Then the mysterious hooded man hit the other man with not one, nor two but three short lefts.

For a long while the two men stood above their victims gasping for air. They finally moved away from the unconscious bodies and towards the deep well Brook Ward had constructed. Using the long tin plate ladle, Johnny scooped some water from a bucket which rested on top of the solid stone wall and drank. The hooded man edged closer to the fence poles and stared down at the still dazed gunman.

'We'd better hogtie these men.'

Johnny nodded in agreement.

'Then we gotta get that dang chestnut mare off Gene's leg.'

'Come on.' The masked man tossed a rope from off the fence poles to the young cowboy. 'We'd better start roping these rats before they come to.'

'Reckon these critters might sing us a nice song when they wake up?' Johnny started to tie the rope around one of the bush-whacker's boots before running the rope up and around the bleeding man's neck and then down around his wrists.

'All we need is for them to point a finger in Rufas Johnson's direction,' the Red Roan Rider said coldly as his magnificent stallion rounded the corner of the house and trotted up beside them. The hooded man took a rope off the silver-topped saddle horn and began walking towards the two stricken men lying before the front of the farmhouse porch. Johnny Puma kept pace with the man in crimson who had filled their enemies with so much terror and knelt to assist him tying them together.

'Where did you get a horse like that?' Johnny asked staring across at the handsome steed.

'He kinda adopted me,' the strange man shrugged.

The night was still only half way through when Tomahawk walked out from the illuminated farmhouse carrying a fresh pot of coffee and began refilling the tin cups of his pensive friends as they sat waiting for all three of their prisoners to awaken.

'Why we waiting, Gene?' the old timer asked as he rested the heavy pot at his feet.

Gene Adams was still rubbing his leg trying to get it to come back to life. 'I wanna hear what these critters have to say for themselves.'

'But why?' Tomahawk shook his head and sipped at the black beverage. 'The Red Roan Rider rounded up our horses and the pack mule. Your stupid chestnut mare is now back up on her feet, so how come we don't go and do what we set out to do?'

'Maybe Gene Adams is a man who never allows anger to obscure his actions, Tomahawk,' said the voice from behind the mask.

All three of the Bar 10 men looked at the man who guarded his secrets well and nodded. Even when he spoke they were no wiser to his true voice. He could have been of any age. There was no clue in his tone. Nothing but well placed words stating facts with little obvious emotion attached to them. He leaned against the wall next to the other men and yet never allowed his true identity to show.

'How come you showed up here, stranger?' Johnny asked as he watched the steam rising off the rim of his cup.

'I knew you were coming here and I figured there might be a reception party waiting for you,' the rider replied.

'I for one am mighty grateful you decided to help,' Adams said stomping his numb leg onto the ground every other word.

'Me too, son,' Tomahawk raised his cup and winked at the masked man.

'I think now we oughta act, Adams,' the Red Roan Rider said bluntly pointing at the pack mule tied to the corral fence posts. 'You bought that dynamite to do a job and I'll help you do that job.'

'We still got us time before sun-up.' Adams nodded at the strange crimson clothed man.

'Reckon we ain't got nothing to worry about with you on our side, friend,' Johnny said sipping at the strong brew looking at the Red Roan Rider admiringly.

The hooded man did not appear as confident as the youthful Bar 10 cowboy beside him. He simply lowered his head and brooded thoughtfully whilst the three prisoners who were roped together began to make their anger evident.

'The back shootin' vermin are stirring, Gene,' Tomahawk noticed pointing down at their tethered prey. 'I still reckon we should have plugged them like they was intending to plug us.'

'We'll just let the law sort these men out, Tomahawk,' Adams finished his coffee and tossed the empty tin cup to his old friend. 'And if Tiberius Fox wants to borrow a few Bar 10 ropes I'm sure we'd be happy to lend them to him.'

'As long as they use them to lynch these critters.' Tomahawk waved his axe angrily at the hogtied men.

Adams stood and towered over the trash at his feet.

'Now maybe we'll get us some answers.'

EIGHTEEN

The four very different riders had two options. One was to attempt riding in through the well-guarded main gates which still sported at least six highly paid marksmen and the other choice was to use the dried up river-bed. Adams chose the latter. All he truly wanted to do was blast the dam sky high and send the water back down into the parched land south of Johnson's spread. As the four riders made their way along the rim of the Nueces River with the moonlight on their spines, Adams kept on thinking of the words spoken to them by their prisoners back on the Ward ranch. The men kept telling of the treasure Johnson had been searching so desperately for. How the Chinese slave labour had already pulled out a few necklaces encrusted with precious gems and a few odd golden coins from the mud at the base of the wooden dam.

Father Gonzales had also spoken of the treasure and yet it had seemed ludicrous to think it might still be there after so many years. Yet it was still there and this was the only thing which motivated the ruthless fat man. Johnson must have spent an entire fortune seeking another one. There was an insanity about it. Adams had no idea what would drive a man into such a single-minded avenue of avarice. If there was one sin Gene Adams had never experienced, it was greed. To him it made no sense.

Reining in the weary chestnut, the Bar 10 rancher stared down from their high vantage point at the mud which now appeared blue in the light of the new moon. It was churned up far more than when he had been here with Tomahawk, he thought.

'What's wrong, Gene?' Johnny asked as his pinto pony moved next to the tall mare.

'Does that mud seem a mite dug up to you, Johnny?'

'A tad, but you told me them Chinese were digging it up when you came here with Tomahawk,' the youngster replied.

The old timer edged his quarter horse next to the three other mounts and stared down at the muddy river-bed below the dam.

'I see what you mean, Gene. There weren't no deep holes like that when we came here.'

'Those are really big holes. Almost like graves.' Adams rubbed his gloved hands over his tired face.

'Maybe they are graves!' Tomahawk gasped.

'Or just where treasure chests have been removed, boys,' Adams thought aloud. 'An awful lot of treasure chests by the look of it.'

The Red Roan Rider pulled his stallion around and stared along both sides of the river-bank.

'Where are the sentries? This place is usually crawling with Johnson's riflemen.'

'Old Roan here is right. There ain't one man on sentry duty, boys,' Adams noted nervously.

'I don't like it.'

'Neither do I, Johnny,' Tomahawk gulped. 'I smells me a trap.'

Adams blew out heavily at the cold night air. His leg still hurt and blurred his judgement.

'Trap or not, we came here to do a job and we ain't leaving until it's done.'

Tapping their spurs gently into the flesh of their horses, the four riders slowly descended the dry crumbling embankment towards the floor of the river-bed cautiously leading the pack mule behind them. Along the edge of the dried up river the ground was solid but as they drew closer to the massive dam, made of countless felled trees, it grew ever softer beneath their horses' hooves. All four horsemen felt the cool chill of the dam as it groaned under the strain of holding back a million gallons of trapped river water.

'Keep your eyes peeled, boys.' Adams advised over his broad shoulder.

It was the sound of a gun hammer being cocked which caused the bloodshot eyes of Rufas Johnson to open from the depths of his slumbers and stare out into the dark bedroom. A slumber which was bathed in the dreams filled with Spanish golden bullion bars plus a million jewels and all the joys which only boundless wealth could manufacture.

Yet now he could smell his own fear overwhelming him as he lay beneath the expensive sheets afraid to move a muscle. Lying quite still, he heard the footsteps drawing closer to him across the well-polished floor. The sound of spurs followed each step as Johnson trembled beneath his bed linen.

Then through the small gap beside his head he caught sight of the figure approaching as its image traced across his long dressing mirror. Sweat ran down Johnson's face and from every pore of his portly body as he tried to see through the gap in the sheets. Whoever it was, continued moving quietly closer with a cocked pistol in his raised hand. A pistol trained upon the bed.

With only the light of a candle flickering upon his bedside table to help him see, Johnson knew it was a futile exercise. As the intruder closed in on the bed, the sweating fat man tried to think which of his men would be bold enough to kill him. The day long brandy drinking made even this simple question totally unfathomable.

All Rufas Johnson could do was to reach beneath one of his plump feather pillows and attempt to locate the pistol he always kept there. Johnson's hand slid underneath his pillows and his large swollen fingers stretched around until they finally located the mother of pearl grip of his Smith & Wesson Frontier .44. Like its owner, it was clumsy and ugly, but perfect for hiding in such places. Ready, should the need ever arise, for self-protection.

With his heart pounding frantically, Rufas Johnson tried to retrieve the heavy weapon without the approaching assassin noticing any sign of movement which might cause him to start shooting before Johnson had his own firearm cocked and readied.

Soaked in his own stinking sweat, the large man used his long fingernails and finally was able to drag the weapon into his wet hand. Then, as his thumb managed to pull the hammer back until it engaged beneath the muffling effects of the bed linen, the shadow of the intruder covered Johnson's pillow. Through one eye, the large man could see the intruder's gun being raised at waist level and aimed straight at his face.

Without breathing, Johnson slid his own weapon around from beneath his double chin and levelled the barrel straight at the man's groin. He had never fired this gun before and it scared him as to what would happen when he squeezed the trigger beneath the sheets. He had spent a lifetime and a small fortune paying others to do his killing for him until this moment. For the first time it was he who would have to kill or be killed. There was no price tag which could be paid to excuse this action.

The sound of gunfire bounced off the expensively decorated walls of the room along with blood and sinew. The smell of burning cloth filled the nostrils of the survivor.

Burl Nunn walked out of his employer's bedroom still holding his cocked Colt .45 firmly in a hand frozen by shock. As he moved out onto the well-illuminated landing, he staggered and finally looked down at what was left of his groin. He had lost all of which men such as he spent their lives boasting about. Blood was spurting out from his stained pants like a fountain of scarlet covering the highly polished floorboards. He still had not felt the pain as he leaned on the railing which circled the high landing and balanced over the hallway below. A hallway filled with the five wooden treasure chests all opened and all displaying the fortune in gold and jewels they had so long concealed. Dropping the pistol, he began to shake as he watched his life's blood pouring from his wound down through the railings and splashing on the distant fortune below. It was a sickening sight even for one such as Nunn. For a hundred and fifty years the riches contained inside those ancient boxes had not seen the light of day and now his blood was masking their gleaming beauty once more.

'Why, Burl? Why?' Rufas Johnson's hysterical voice screamed out from the doorway behind him.

Nunn rested his hands upon the rail and managed to turn his head to stare blankly at the rotund man whose face was covered in the blood which had splattered over him when he had pulled the trigger on the Smith & Wesson. Blood which dripped off his jowls onto his once pristine nightshirt.

'Why what, boss?' Nunn coughed as blood ran from his mouth.

Johnson stepped closer to the man, who no longer had what most men prided themselves in.

'You came into my room to kill me. Why?'

Nunn sagged and found his legs no longer willing or able to support his weight. Sliding onto his rear the pain raced through him causing him to scream.

'You tried to kill me, Burl?' Johnson stepped closer to the man sitting in the pool of his own blood. A pool which grew larger with every beat of his heart, which was pumping his life away.

'I never gave it no thought, Rufas.' Nunn spat out the choking red phlegm and rested his hand upon the pistol he had dropped a few seconds earlier. 'All the time we was sending them damn Chinese down to dig, I never gave it no mind. Then they find the chests, just like you said they would. Still I never gave it no mind until we cracked them chests open and I set eyes upon all that gold and those jewels.'

Johnson's bare feet stepped through the blood covered flooring as he drew closer to the man he had known for more years than he could recall.

'You wanted to take the money for yourself?'

Nunn allowed his fingers to encircle the weapon at his side and slowly his index finger slid around its trigger.

'Guess it's what they call gold fever.'

'I would have shared it with you.' Johnson's eyes could not believe the destruction his single bullet had created and tried to avoid staring at the wound. Yet wherever he looked, blood was everywhere and still pumping out from the lap of his stricken gunhand.

'Why should I have taken a mere share when I could take it all, you fat bastard?' Nunn raised his Colt and squeezed the trigger.

The bullet tore its way through the portly Johnson and sent him falling backwards. Johnson gave out a last huge gasp as his head rolled over.

Dragging himself up onto his feet, Burl Nunn leaned over the railings and cast his eyes upon the glittering vision below.

The sound of the explosion coming from the direction of the dam shook the huge house violently causing the massive chandelier hanging from the vaulted ceiling above the hall to come crashing down spilling its dozens of lighted candles in all directions around the luxurious house. Nunn pulled himself to his full height and stared down at the scene. As the flames took hold of the furniture and window drapes, and smoke began to swirl upward, the gunslinger raised his pistol up until it was aiming into his mouth.

From the safety of their vantage point high above the embankment, the four riders held onto the reins of their terrified mounts as the ground continued to tremble. They watched as the river water flowed through the destroyed dam down along its natural route. A route carved out by nature over a million years.

'Now Sanora will be able to live again,' the Red Roan Rider said, spinning his stallion around.

Gene Adams pulled his reins and followed the roan.

'Now we better go and pay Johnson a visit.'

Tomahawk drew his black quarter horse level with the two larger mounts as Johnny trotted along beside him.

'What's that?' the eagle eyed youngster asked, pointing directly ahead of them.

The sky glowed brightly as the flames from Johnson's blazing house licked the heavens.

'Sun up,' Tomahawk sniffed.

'That ain't the sun rising you old fool!' Adams snapped as he stood in his stirrups vainly trying to see.

'Something's on fire!' Johnny shouted over the sound of the raging river behind them.

'Something big,' Adams agreed.

'It must be the Johnson house!' the hooded rider exclaimed. 'Come on.'

The four riders spurred their mounts and thundered along the dark trail. With every stride the smell of smoke grew greater in their nostrils. As they cleared the rise, the full extent of the fire was clear. Never had any of the quartet seen such a fire before. The flames seemed to be trying to burn the very stars themselves.

As the four riders led by Gene Adams approached the blazing house, they heard a shot coming from within the inferno.

Adams reined his chestnut in hard and sat watching in disbelief as the shell of the huge house crumbled into mere ashes. The intense heat forced the riders to stay well clear of the destruction before them. Adams dismounted when he saw the caged faces of the Chinese slaves illuminated by the intense fire and, rushing to the small structure which had been in total contrast to the edifice Johnson had created for himself, the Bar 10 rancher shot the lock off and pulled the door wide open freeing the be-draggled men.

'Beat it. You're free,' Adams said to the bruised and dirty Orientals.

Suddenly the remainder of Johnson's once

mighty force came from out of the shadows firing their Winchesters frantically.

The Red Roan Rider rode straight at the small group of men and leapt from his saddle taking two of them down heavily.

Johnny drew one of his guns and began shooting at the men who were trying real hard to kill them. With his usual accuracy, he brought two men down before his pony reared and he fell from his saddle dazing himself.

Tomahawk watched as one of the guards closed in on Adams before pulling his hatchet from his belt and throwing it with all his might. The axe hit the man high, splitting his head wide open. Adams turned on his heels and gave the old man a smile as he tossed the tomahawk back to him.

'I still got the touch, Gene.'

'That you have, old timer,' Adams said rushing to meet the last of their attackers square on. Ducking a wide right, then an equally wide left, Adams smashed his gloved fists into the face of the gunman, sending him rolling over amid the burning ashes which were falling like rain around the scene, before finishing him off with a blow from one of his gold-plated pistols.

Swinging about on his heels again, Adams noticed their masked companion wrestling with the two heavily built sentries. Signalling to Tomahawk, the white-haired rancher began heading for the trio of fighting men, whilst the old man rode past him and clubbed one of the guards with his axe.

Then the hooded man pulled his opponent up by his shirt collar and smashed his left fist into his face. The man fell helplessly onto the ground at Adams's feet as he arrived.

'Good punch, Roan,' Adams gasped.

'What took you so long?' the masked man said plucking his Stetson up off the ground and placing it over his hooded head.

'I got me a real bad leg, sonny,' Adams grinned.

Tomahawk slid from his saddle and wiped

the blood from his hatchet before pushing it into his belt.

'Reckon it's over?'

Gene Adams turned and watched as Johnny came walking towards them muttering under his breath as he beat the dust off the seat of his jeans.

'I wonder what happened here, boys?'

'I guess we'll never know, Gene,' Tomahawk bristled.

'One thing's for sure … Johnson would have hanged if he hadn't have died in that blaze,' Adams frowned.

'Can we be sure he did?' Tomahawk asked.

'He was in that house all right. Otherwise his men wouldn't have still been here,' Adams said pulling his gloves tight over his hands.

The hooded man whistled and his red roan stallion trotted up to him. Grasping the silver saddle horn the man mounted and bowed to the three Bar 10 men.

'You leaving?' Adams asked.

'Our job here is done, my friends,' the man

said jabbing his spurs into the sides of his roan and riding out into the darkness.

Adams looked at his two friends and rested an arm around each of their shoulders.

'My leg is killing me, boys.'

'You're lucky it's only your leg,' Johnny said, rubbing his rear where he had landed.

FINALE

Bessie Ward stood staring out at her land. A land which was now beginning to show signs of the great river's return. The tall figure of Gene Adams knelt and plucked a small flower from off the soil and handed it to the silent woman as they headed back towards the farmhouse.

'Feel the roots, Bessie,' Adams grinned. 'Moist.'

'I can see the difference already, Gene,' she nodded. 'Even the air smells sweeter.'

Adams walked up to the hitching rail and untied his reins.

'Some men are real strange critters, Bessie. They value useless trinkets and risk everything, including their lives to gain more and more useless trinkets. Yet on a land such as this, only water is of real value.

It's precious. Without it everything dies.'

'Thanks to you we have our most precious gift back.' Bessie squeezed his gloved hand before watching as he gripped his saddlehorn and mounted the chestnut mare slowly beside Tomahawk who was waiting patiently.

'This is a good ranch, Bessie,' Adams said nodding.

'It will take a long time to get our herd back.'

'When I get back to the Bar 10, I'll get my boys to cut out a young bull and fifty longhorns. I'll send them down here for you.'

'But I have no money, Gene.'

'Like I said before. Some men value trinkets. I'm not one of those men.' Adams stared over his shoulder as the young Johnny walked back to the house with Anita on his arm.

'I was telling Bessie that I'm gonna send down a small herd for her and Anita to restart this ranch, Johnny.' Adams grinned at the young man who managed to tear his lips away from the beautiful female before stepping into his stirrup and mounting his pinto.

'Can I bring the herd here, Gene?' Tomahawk asked.

Johnny glanced down at the lovely blushing female before tapping Adams's shoulder.

'I figure it would be a job for a much younger man, Gene.'

'A younger man?' Adams's eyebrows raised as he tilted a look at the cowboy. 'I wonder exactly what age you reckon would be the right one for such a job, Johnny?'

'About my age,' Johnny smiled.

'You're sure you wouldn't mind heading a trail drive back here, Johnny?' Adams teased. 'I'd hate for you to come all the way back here for nothing.'

'Oh, it wouldn't be for nothing, Uncle Gene,' Anita said fluttering her long tempting lashes.

Gene Adams leaned back in his saddle

and roared with laughter as he turned his horse away from the house and raised an arm to the two Ward women bidding them farewell.

'Adios, lovely ladies!' Adams laughed as he and his two friends headed away from the house.

'Did you ever figure out who that Red Roan Rider was, Gene?' Tomahawk asked as the three riders headed along the trail which was already beginning to turn green as fresh grass shoots were sprouting up in all directions.

'Sure did,' Adams grinned.

'Then who was he?' the old timer asked as they headed north back to the Bar 10.

'It was obvious. You must have noticed.'

'Noticed what, Gene?'

'He was a southpaw. A lefty.' Adams laughed. 'Did you happen to notice back in Sanora who was also a lefty?'

Johnny and Tomahawk both looked at each other as they rode beside the tall Texan.

'Come on, Gene. Tell us!' both men begged.

Gene Adams continued riding and laughing for another fifty miles whilst wondering whether or not he would tell his closest friends the secret. The more they begged for the answer the more the rancher began to enjoy the situation. After all, it was a long ride back to the Bar 10.

The publishers hope that this book has given you enjoyable reading. Large Print Books are especially designed to be as easy to see and hold as possible. If you wish a complete list of our books please ask at your local library or write directly to:

Dales Large Print Books
Magna House, Long Preston,
Skipton, North Yorkshire.
BD23 4ND

This Large Print Book for the partially sighted, who cannot read normal print, is published under the auspices of
THE ULVERSCROFT FOUNDATION